Misery Luvs

Company

Mistafunn

Misery Luvs Company

By Mistafunn

MiSERY LUVS COMPANY by Mistafunn

Library of Congress Cataloging-in-Publication Data
ISBN: 978-0-9848954-3-4
Funn, Daryl A, a.k.a. mistafunn
Misery Luvs Company / by Mistafunn

FOREWARD

By April "AP" Smith

When asked to describe himself using one word, *awesometaculanificent* was Daryl Funn's answer. I'm sure those of you—while trying to sound this out phonetically—are probably asking yourselves, "What in the world is that"? It is the fusing of three words—awesome, spectacular, and magnificent—into one. If you know Daryl, then, this should come as no surprise. For those of you who don't, well, let's just say he has a large (and sometimes bizarre) imagination.

He's "amazingly creative" with a mind's eye not only good for inventing wacky eight syllable words, but also designing websites, t-shirts, peculiar cartoon characters, and his own card game. He writes and performs his own poems and songs as well, and coaches the Java Monkey poetry slam team in Decatur, Ga. He's a chef too, a husband a father, and writes books with tricky titles like this one, "Misery Loves Company."

Six years in the making and it is finally finished! It speaks the "truth" about relationships, providing us with a positive look at the Black male figure. But don't be fooled. This isn't just any ole book about relationships. It's an experience, literally. While we get caught up in a love triangle and the journey of three friends trying to figure things out, we are provided with several opportunities to be "in the moment." Open your minds and fasten your seatbelts because we're in for a hell of a ride with unexpected twists and turns and a lot of Daryl's fun and *awesometaculansificent* personality sprinkled in-between.

Suggested Playlist

1. Dream On Dreamer – The Brand New Heavies
2. Love Me In A Special Way – DeBarge
3. What You Want – The Roots
4. Dolla Wine – Byron Lee & The Dragonaires
5. I Who Have Nothing – Luther Vandross
6. The Lady in My Life – Michael Jackson
7. U Belong To Me – Ben Tankard
8. The Breeze –
9. Catch 22 – Goaple
10. Without You – Mistafunn™
11. All Blues – Kevin Mahogany
12. For Real – Amel Larrieux
13. Sorrow & Misery – Gemini Slim
14. Nobody Knows You When You're Down and Out - The Gene Harris Quartet
15. Still A friend Of Mine – Incognito
16. Need You Now – Avery* Sunshine
17. Where do We Go From Here – Tweet
18. Body – Mark Whitfield

Graduate of THANK U -

By *Mysary Le Noir*

Allow me to take a moment of my existence to say beauty,
elegance, and grace encamp themselves
about you. From the far reaches of night,
day, and all that is good is the sight of God
a brilliant diamond was lifted from the rubble.

Epitomizing all that was to be a rainbow of gems are released in your
praise
Whether naturally born or connected by
path no greater gift could any child of God ask
As the summer winds echo between fingers
Teachers of my spirit I thank God for you.

Heart like homes make shelter for me and the enduring of
The journey that is much like the last sweet whisper ease
Thank u for allowing me to build
Possibilities from your dreams. in that no island is a man
Through all the seasons your wealth rained like innocent storms of
strength
As I prepare to build my throne and prepare for the new
There has been no greater school than the lifetime I've spent at thank U

*The day before graduation has to be one of, if not the busiest day.
Trying to get things done before family arrives, pre -party planning,
going to grab a quick bite to eat before you get you hair done is even
now mission impossible. The rush of needing to get it done right now
and there is no time to even exhale, is often what drives us to brilliance
or insanity. The line between the two is blurred by her conflicting got
to be there and totally not wanting to be stopped by the police.*

*Mysary turns the corner of Madison and Gilmore in her deep blue 4
Runner, jamming to some Cuban rhythms. Pulling in front of a small
semi-detached house, she grabs the bag from the passenger seat and
quickly makes her way to the door. Neecie, a 25 year old hair stylist
and mother of two, has turned half of her home into a hair salon.
There are a few regulars there already, Kia 23, Janet 22, and Toni 25.
Coco 21, Neecie' s younger sister, assists with the business. As Miz
walks in, all eyes turn toward her. Of course Janet sarcastically is the
first to speak.*

Janet: Hey Miss Thing, look what the cat drug in.

Mysary: Janet this ain't the time or the place. Hey Coco, Kia, Toni.
(*Face to face with Neecie giving her a hug.*) What up girl, sorry I'm
late.

Neecie: Miz, you been coming here for how long? , You ain't neva
been on time. Lets get started. You did bring the color you wanted
right? So it's finally here, Graduation Day? I'm so proud of you,
[Clutching her chest] it seems like only yesterday I was putting in
highlights. You all growed up. sniff! sniff!

6

Looking as if to say Girl you are ill with her head under the water. The topic of discussion changes to a more pressing issue. Neecie has been putting money away to eventually open her own salon and turn her house back into a home.

Neecie: So have you heard anything about that property downtown?

Mysary: Yeah! Remind me to give you her number before I leave. When I told her your plans she said it sounded like something she could work with. You know I talked you up good? Her name is Ardella King she wants to look over your business proposal to show to her company. Just a little inside info she told me you already got the property though.

Neecie: Don't play. You serious, don't make me get to shoutin'

Mysary: Fa' real I told her you had a full 3 to 5 year business plan and you had a little money saved up and she was blown away. So many people come up to her with a visions and no thought, expecting the million-dollar dream.

Neecie: God ain't raise no fool now. Thanks girl for everything. Hallelujah (*in loud hush*).

Everyone stops to look at Neecie getting her dance on. Now that Miz's hair is washed and being hand dried by Neecie we turn to a conversation already in progress.

Janet: Yeah girl he read this beautiful poem over the radio. He's s'pposed to be taking her to this dinner theatre ova there on Ritchie Highway.

Coco: Where'd she meet this one?

Toni: A better question, how is the sex?

Janet: She met him on the subway on her way to work.

From under the towel Mysary can barely hear the conversation as she interjects.

Mysary: Hey you guys, Chris wanted me to invite you all to Shelia's next Saturday.

Kia: (*in a snobby upper class voice.*) Let me see next Saturday I have the trip to Tarjay and then there is that sware' at Wally World. Looks like i'm free.

Coco: I think I'll wear my gold halter with my white caprise.

Neecie: CAPRiSE! With all that wagon you dragging. You can't be serious.

Janet: She just betta not try that…(simpering down to a whisper) nonsense, ya heard?

Coco: (Looking at Janet intently) Anna Mae…

And you know how these things go. First you start quoting one movie and before you know it somebody done shouted "You told Harpo ta beat me?" and laughter rains down heavy on a hot spring morning. Alas, Neecie has done her magic once again. Shifting focus Janet starts putting in work on a time bomb just ready to blow. Neecie is curling Miz's hair.

Janet: So Miz, is Darik gonna be at Sheila's? (*With the inflection in her voice so suggestive it almost stilled the room*).

Miz detecting the underlying purpose, refused to engage in a battle of wits with someone so unprepared. However, Neecie ain't the one to be played with.

Neecie: And what's that s'pposed to mean?

Janet: Hey don't crucify me I just wanted to know if ol' girl was going to be with us or be with her man whichever one it may be.

Eyes cut with intensity and bite, as all emotions are laid behind a truly calculated response.

Mysary: In order for me to dignify your slim witted nature with as much as an eye twitch, I would literally have to become void of any common sense and still I would fall short of the verbage that you could adequately comprehend with any type of minimal understanding. Now if you ever question me again about anything oh be sure comprehension is be the least of your worries.

9

Looking as if she is at a loss for words, Kia comes to the rescue by turning up the radio that is playing the classic springtime jam. The majority gets into the groove wiggling and twirling in their seats. Pretty soon the conflict resolution is more of a stand off by each woman going her way. As the song ends Neecie puts the finishing touches on Miz.

Neecie: (taking a bow as she turns Miz around to face the mirror) Thank you! Thank You, you all are too kind.

Everyone staring at her as if to say, "OKAY."

Mysary: Thanks girl. What do I owe you?

Neecie: Just knock'em dead at graduation *(They hug)*

Mysary opening her eyes and noticing how late it is, she quickly breaks the embrace.

Mysary: I told Darik I'd meet him at 12:00. I gotta go. Thanks again for everything! Luv you girl!

Neecie: Luv you too, now go and don't keep that man waitin'. Oh don't forget that phone number.

Mysary: Glad, you reminded me, *(Scribbling on a piece of paper)* here you go.

Hugging everyone as she leaves. Janet and her share a mutual look that says "lata". Out the door again she hops back into her ride and jets off. Her destination to, pick up the graduation dress that needed a few alterations and the shoes. At the first stop light Miz pops in one of her pastor's message on relationships.

"...I don't know about most of you. Some of yall folks are so spiritual you are no earthly good. Just flyin' right past God; all caught up in yourself. Excuse me; we interrupt this existence for a special bulletin brought to you in part by supporters for radical change. Stop letting the lack of luv from your past cock block your future. Yeah, I said cock block, it seems like the only way to get your attention. Oh! Yall wanna take this message to the club then, some of yall still got the stamp on your hand from last night. Don't act like you don't know. You must understand that to be intimate with someone you must know what the word means. Into –leave current surroundings for the cover of a new setting Mate – a union that by all accounts was made to produce something. Last time I checked, intimacy means get into me and see what I see. So if we get intimate we have to see the same thing. The problem is some of yall, as the old folks used to say, are a little cock-eyed. You really need to know who you are first and foremost. The only way to do that is through God. Knowing who you are when someone asks you the question about where you are going or what is your plan, even if you don't have all the answers you can effectively tell them what you see. You need to spend time with you first in order to get a handle on that. Listen, nobody wants to be left alone with themselves, because that means you would have to face your own personal inadequacies. Let me be honest with you, as your pastor I attend an anger management course every Monday. What? I'm not so

11

big that I don't admit as a man I don't have it all together. I don't stand before you expecting you to follow or idolize me. We are in this walk together. I will let this church fall before I let this walk become a 40 year journey. We, me included, are God's people. I am not the shepherd, your spiritual father, or any of the nonsense you heard at some other church. Here, we speak the uncompromised word of God. Debate it how you like. If it doesn't line up with the word, then it wont be done. Now, as I was saying, the reason most of you flow from this one to that one, trying to fill that void, is because you're insatiable. If I tell it like it should be, most of you would want me hung because you don't want to stop. Men want that quick nut and that's it. Oh, don't act like a prude now. Some women want that steamy love, while some of you are worst than men, just give me the hit and get to stepping. Where is the fulfillment in that?..."

Druid Hill Park, right across from the reservoir, we see Christopher finishing up his water as his continues to write in his journal. 18 hours till graduation and the pressure to resolve even the simplest thing is frustrating. Then again, this is the start of the last summer, but the beginning of the change. Do you finally say what you could not in 1,465 days since the start of all this grown folks feelings? It was easier when you were middle school buddies but now it's so different.

Not far from home but nowhere close to reality, he drowns himself in the smothering breeze of confused thoughts. Finally realizing he came here to clear his mind, Christopher looks at the to-do list and in an attempt to complete something, returns to the bands play list for the show at Shelia's in two weeks. How did he get so off track? Was it the tune playing over and over in his head? Could it be the frustration of being the only male in his class that is not in the business yet and no prospects on the horizon or is it her? The gorgeous and maddening resistance that has us wallowing in delight of fear. Fear is the only unknown that can love you into the arms of destruction or triumph.

The sun sprinkles between the leaves to catch a hint of his glasses. With his head deeply buried in thought, the distant shouts of a woman have no effect. Hung up on the rhythm for the end of a tune, he fails to notice a huge cinnamon brown Doberman heading straight for him. Trailed behind this mammoth, a young lady tries breathlessly to command the attention of the dog first. As that fails she focuses on trying to gain Chris's attention. Snapped back to reality as if pounded in the face, his sight is plastered with the view of this dog barreling toward him. Unable to move Chris sits motionless gripping his pen to the point of snapping it in two. Heart racing fast enough to win the triple-crown in one swoop, he tries to pray for the Lord's intervention. A tongue-waging storm of dust and muscles zooms past to the opposing side of the tree where the thunderous sound of relief hits the base. You know what we do after a situation like this. Wiping the brow with a deep sigh, Chris counts his blessings only to have the moment broken by that same dog coming around with a look of relief. Recognizing this dog poses no threat to life, Chris reaches out to stroke the back of his head. Looking to see his collar or name tag, the somewhat playful pooch bounces around. With his weight tipping the scales at about 75 to 80 pounds this behavior can quickly become an appetite for destruction. Able to somewhat settle the mammoth down Chris and the dog engage in friendly banter.

Chris: Yeah, I know how you feel son.

Taking a seat next to Chris, a winded woman approaches feeling the wait of her emotion, the dog quickly falls to a humble and cute belly crawl.

Maya: (*out of breath for the moment*) Out of all the trees in this park what is so special about this one. Keno, I know you hear me talking to you. You are definitely in for it when we get home.

Chris: Maybe this is the only one that said boys?

Maya: (*finally regaining her breath*) I'm sorry. Are you okay? I don't know what got into him. He has never done anything like that before. He didn't mess up anything did he? Keno get over here, mommy's not mad come on.

Keno walks slowly toward her with his head low, eyes looking up in calculated sorrow. Chris grabs a water from his shoulder sack and offers it as he stands dusting off his pants.

Chris: You look like you could use this.

Maya: Thanks. Oh, I apologize. I'm Maya, Maya Luv but everybody calls me Mai for short.

Chris: Christopher Company.

Maya: Nice to meet you.

Chris: Same here. Maya Luv is it? That's an interesting name.

Mai: I've heard the jokes and yes it makes relationships interesting.

Chris: (*baffled for a moment*) What?

Mai: Most guys make some statement about the name "Mai Luv". You know clowning about that Mary J. song.

Chris: Never that. (*Laughing as he finishes packing his bag*)

Mai: I see you are a writer or something. Let me guess, you are one of those neo-soul brothas writing that epic luv poem of God and mother earth right? (*With a ginger smile she awaits a response*)

Chris: Nah, writing is my luv. No pun intended and in this city with the way things are, this is one of the only places I can find peace. You know, without having to go up to the mountains on some spiritual quest or something. I need to hear the melody of the song or piece.

Mai: Interesting

Chris: Would you like to hear it?

Mai: Sure. You don't need to give a precursor or a disclaimer or something?

The way his eyes take hold of me commanded all of my attention. Wow, nobody's ever done that before. He's cute, okay so let's guess what the problem is. No rings, nicely dressed and nails a little rough.

15

Chris: Nah, we straight. It is untitled though (*clearing his throat*).

The porcelain bed where she laid denied
me any possible means of escape.
Her passionate purr of scented heat
blesses my face with kisses.

Eyes embrace every part of her form
Slowly breaking each breath into a stuttered exhale
it's nothing like getting some piping hot
goodness early in the morning.

Strong fingers pierce pores releasing
The aroma of delectability
Nothing of caffeinated falsified pleasure
Could come close to the release upon insertion.

Never as good as the first time
but there is joy in repetition. Joy in repetition.
(*short pause*) Joy in repetition,

As square sun drops melt between her soft brown layers
A honey and maple cover blankets her nakedness.

Wanting this right now moist thoughts marinade my lips
Convincing my tongue to do butterfly colored backstrokes
I begin before the taste could behave as usual
The once pure moment was defiled by the imitation.

Deep in my heart I knew it was wrong
I could no longer continue.

How could I do this to her, she's been so good to me
Could i ever be forgiven for this great wrong?
I'll never make pancakes when the Mrs. Butterworth is gone.

Looking like "Oh my God", no you didn't just do a sexy pancake poem. With a tender smile, his eyes lasso her face connecting for a unique moment, neither could deny what they started to feel but they hesitate and break the moment before they could get lost.

Mai: Cute and funny. I likes.

Chris: Oh I gots the looks and the laughs? I take it you meant the poem.

Mai: Oh, you sportin' a little somethin', something too. So if you don't mind me asking and I hope I am not being to forward, what does your girl think of you going off on these spiritual quest or is getting away from her the peace you mean?

Chris: If there were one, she would have to understand sometimes a little distance helps keep the fire going. You know what I mean? (*Delayed in thought, he catches on that she is investigating his current relationship status. Unable to capitalize on the moment internally down he lets it pass*).

Mai: Yeah.

As a quiet laugh is shared something deeper is exchanged. It could be the sweet smell of honeysuckle plants or the soft breeze that reminds you of the beauty of spring or it could be that look that two people share that just speaks volumes without saying anything. As if on cue the stuttering beep of his watch and the tune of her phone break into a strange overlapping harmony; as a unison "I gotta..." blends in.

17

Mai: 'Scuse me for a second would you? Hello? Hey let me hit you right back aight? Okay, then I'll be there in 20 minutes. Thanks, bye. Sorry about that, you were saying?

Chris: Well I see you gotta be out. Me too. Before graduation tonight, some friends and I are planning a little party at my place. Maybe you could stop by? I mean, if that's not being too forward?

Mai: Congrats. (*Hmm, it seems there is a lot to learn about you Mr. Company.*) I don't do the party scene too much and I'll probably be at work late tonight too. How bout I call you after work and we go for coffee or something if you are still up? I wouldn't want you to be late for graduation now would I?

Chris: Interesting.

Mai: What?

Chris: A woman who knows exactly what she wants and not afraid to go after it.

Mai: That doesn't threaten you does it?

Chris: Nah, it's good. So where do you work?

Mai: Downtown at the Narthex Building.

Chris: You on your way there now?

Mai: I have take care of a few things first but yeah. Why?

Chris: No real reason, just my graduation rehearsal is not that far away at Symphony Hall. To be honest, I don't want this conversation to end. I was going to say, if you had some time, maybe we could get some tea or something?

Mai: So what if I would've said I work out near The Plaza (*with a hint of jovial sarcasm*)? What then? You would have come up with some story about how the party decoration place is not to far and...

Chris: Ok, you got me. What can I say?

Mai: Don't worry we will talk again.

Chris: Oh, I know that.

Mai: Oh my, confident aren't we?

Chris: And you know this. Well, you have to go and I do need to hit the spot before I roll out and make sure things are in place for tonight. So we'll talk later?

Mai: You will be bogged down so much with family and friends and trying to get yourself situated. You may not have time for me. I understand, just let it be known that I don't like my attention interrupted.

Chris: On the real shorty, hit me up about 9:30 or 10, if you are done with work. I got your attention?

Mai: Interesting.

Her gentle smile plays back the friendly banter placing the ball in his court. Quickly he responds.

Chris: What?

They both laugh seemingly at the same thing. Stopping to look at one another the laughter continues and fades to smiles.

Mai: So I must have made a good impression.

Chris: Why you say that?

Mai: ...You're willing to give up partying with your friends for little ol' me.

Chris: My grandfather told me "if good things come to those who wait, who gets the great things in life?".

Mai: So this right here is a great thing?

Chris: That's a bet. Look we both need to be out and I could keep this going. So where are you parked?

Mai: Over on the other side of that hill.

Chris: I'm headed that way too. I stay over there off Madison and Harlem. You think Keno would mind if I walked you to your car? (*You know how it is, you meet that honey and you try to make every second stretch.*)

Mai: C'mon boy. Pulling the leash in a gesture to motion it's time to go. He says you can come too.

Chris: Cool.

Mai: You seem pretty lax being that you about to graduate I mean...

Chris: Nah, never that. All I had to get done today was the do and as you clearly stated earlier, I'm on point with mine. So I need to finish up the house for the party and then its on to graduation.

She really begins to feel that confidence in Christopher and wonders if any of this is real. Attractions like this don't happen unless written in the pages of some love story. She's waiting in an anxious rest for the other shoe to fall. He has a girlfriend or two, he has kids that he doesn't see, he lives at home with his mom, or everything he just said was a lie to just to get to know me. Thinking that there are no real good men anymore. You can see the invisible scars of past relationships molding her apprehension. With good reason, we all have been in a relationship where the person moved into our hearts and once everything was ove,r they forgot to take the promises they left there.

Finally reaching her car and a few blocks from his house they stand there. They are two abbreviated questions wanting the other to answer.

21

Silent jitters, a little nerves, and smiles, spring explode back and forth quick enough to make memorable impressions. Realizing they both really need to go they reach to hug?

This is what purity taste like; minds harmonize in one moment and retreat to surface laughter but internally screaming WOOOOOW! The hug from him created so much comfort she could only relax in every sense of the word. Her embrace laid the invitation to get to know the real her if he really wanted to. In apprehension of giving away too much, they both release in harmony.

Chris: It was really nice meeting you. Amazing hug. So talk to you later?

Mai: Indeed. I got to do something special for Keno tonight.

Chris: Send a little piece of that from me. Thanks dawg, good looking out.

Keno from the back seat curled his huge frame around his pull toy not even acknowledging their existence. Her car door open he stands on the opposite side they try to leave but that flirtatious attraction is stronger than they even know. Taking charge Chris releases the nonverbal hold on the moment. Turning to walk away he hears the car door close and then in a moment, the engine starts. Of course she is checking him out. He wants to turn around but that might look too desperate or she may stop and then they are back to pauses in time to momenst of looks and smiles. Chris walks down the road singing until he reaches the house.

Checking the mailbox in her sports bra, baggy sweats rolled at the waist, iPod strapped to her arm, Airicka hums what often seems to be, her epigram singing the hook as if some sort of release.

Airicka: *Love me in a special way. What more can I say, Love me now! Love me in a special way. What more can i say, Love Me Now...*

Chris walking up to the mailbox about the same time with that normal look of "Oh,Brother, not this song again"

Chris: Anything for me?

She hears him, but at the same time the sweet spot of the song comes up and no one interrupts the most important part of your favorite jam when you're feeling it. Conscious of his presence, fully aware of what his request, she just hands him the three envelopes. Shuffling through the mail as he walks up the porch stairs, he can hear the phone ringing. Airicka, turning down her music before the next tune, listens to see if the phone is for her. Coming to the door phone in hand, Chris holds it up in a way that indicates who it could be. One look of his face and he confirms her thought. Passing the phone like a baton, Airicka squenched her face and smiles at Chris like what?

Aricka: Hey you, what up?

: Nothing much, just wondering what you bout to get into.

Aricka: Bout to jump in the shower

23

: Sounds good to me. You need some company?

Aricka: What would get done? Really?

: Not as much as what, but who. Right?

Airicka: Aren't you supposed to be at work?

: And?

Aricka: What you coming by for a quick wash and wax? I don't do the quick serve and I like my service done right the first time.

: Oh, so what you trying to say?

Airicka: I believe I said it quite clear.

Just then the phone beeps

Airicka: Was that you or me?

: I think it was you?

Airicka: Hold on.

: So am I coming to help or what?

Airicka: Hold on!

Clicking over

Airicka: Hello. Oh hey! Yeah he's here. Give me a second to get off the other line. No hold on, Chris has been waiting for your call.

Clicking back over

Airicka: Hey I gotta go. That is an important call for Chris. You are coming tonight right?

:Yeah, what time again?

Airicka: About 8:30 - 9:00. Later.

:Peace.

Before clicking back Airicka beckons Chris to pick up the line. It's Tischa with nothing new to report on Nate's status, just calling to get a friendly ear. Always the gentlemen, Chris picking up the phone uses this time to make sure Tischa and the family are okay and if there is anything they need. Tischa, a classmate and a member of the band, is the girlfriend of Sam, one of Chris's best friends. Tischa and Chris have grown tight, as most best friends and girlfriends tend to do. You know with girlfriends needing help with birthday surprise gifts and trying to get the pulse of what is going on? Able to shift between thoughts, Chris calculates his words, trying to make sure his well placed jokes provide the comfort a friend needs while making sure he shows his concern with confidence. A member of Tischa's family is having surgery. Nothing serious. However anytime someone goes into the hospital a little part of you tends to worries. Chris's lite humor helps calm her nerves. Sam walks in as Tischa thanks Chris for keeping her company.

Tischa: …Thanks Chris. Sam is here now.

Chris: Cool, T. Let me holla at him.

Tischa: Okay, thanks again.

Chris: Come on, you know we got you.

Sam: What up C?

Chris: Nothing much, I think T is having a hard time but you know how she is, always putting up a front.

Sam: True.

Chris: I just wanted to give you a heads up. I understand if you don't come to the party tonight.

Sam: Yeah, I will see if she needs to get away for a bit. But cool, we may just stay here and talk tonight.

Chris: Well go take care of that woman. If I don't see you tonight you still coming by to pick up me and Airicka at about 1:45 or 2:00 right?

Sam: And you know this. Keep it clean tonight. Don't do anything I've already done.

Chris: Whatever dude! It's the night before graduation. I may be dumb but i'm not stupid.

Sam: Word Son. Holla!

Chris: Atcha, peace!

So Christopher and Airicka spend the rest of the day straightening the house and cooking. Mysary comes home bag full of goods and immediately starts on her duties. Conversations are cut down to overlapping requests and responses, "Did you remember the..., Never mind" and " Where is the... I got it... Almost finished with it." The aromas hypnotize hands to take nibbles[1] while the fresh scent of clean baptizes the air. Of course music is blasting with the windows open wide. In all the hustle, Chris never gets the chance to talk about his day to Airicka or Mysary. Time has moved by so fast as soon as they all had a moment to sit down and breathe the first guest has arrived. Christopher got dressed while the stuffed chicken was baking, so he is responsible for greeting the guest while Airicka and Mysary do the beauty thing.

This night was nothing really big, just a few close friends over for dinner and drinks before the big day. What started out as a simple

---

[1] *Recipes: Lady T's & Sweet Meatballs (p.287) Cucumbers (p.288) Cookies N' Crème Cupcakes (p.289) Cranberry Punch (p.295)*

dinner of 8 - 10 quickly turned into a party of 20 plus. There was Scrabble, Taboo, Scene It, Karaoke, and what would a party be without a game of Spades? Quickly, everyone turn the tables around and it becomes more like a buffet. In the kitchen, Airicka is putting more food out, sampling a little, talking with friends who claim they want to help, and getting side track by the door ringing. Mysary. of course is bartending, when she is pulled to take her turn at one of the game tables. Christopher is in charge of coats and making sure everything in the house is alright. Before people really get into anything the three hosts call everyone together.

Mysary: First of all, we would like to thank you all for coming tonight. We didn't want to do anything really big seeing as how it would be wrong for us to show up late for graduation.

Christopher: Yeah, they would have to start calling the names in reverse order if the A through D's weren't there.

Mysary: ...Especially with the real party at Sheila's tomorrow night.

Party Guest: Yeah. You know this! A'ight!

Mysary: Without making this take any longer, we want to say a quick prayer and lets get to the food, the drinks and the games because we will shut this down at 11! Not 11:01, 11:05, eleven O'ten.

Christopher always quick to catch those slip ups and the only one bold enough to say anything...

28

Chris: Really eleven O'ten? You did just say that, right? Let me pray and you can not have another drink tonight!

Miz: Whatever!

Chris: Dear Heavenly Father, we thank you for this opportunity to come together and fellowship. Thank you Lord for everyone who made the four year or longer journey to get here. In less than 12 hours it will be officially over. Blessed the food we are about to receive and the hands that prepared it. Bless the games and the drinks. Let us all have a good time in You and let us have a great day tomorrow. Get us home safe, before eleven O ten. We ask all these things in Jesus name, Amen.

Party Guests: Amen!

Some return to the games, and the others go for food and a few hit the bar. Small toasts are every where. Jokes run from room to room. Airicka, Mysary, and Christopher are all pulled in different directions, so many people needing different things. When they do get the opportunity to sit and talk it's in pairs, never as the trio that everyone has come to know them as. The later it gets the more fun the party becomes and inevitably people are lessand less inclined to leave. Out of nowhere the one song comes on and like clock work it happens. The traditional soul train line breaks out. You ever wonder what makes this a party favorite just as much as the electric slide is a standard part of the family reunion or any major event involving "FOLKS"? At any event, everyone busts out the Whop, the Cabbage Patch, the Rubiks Cube, the Flinstone, Da Butt, the Freak and it is a virtual wind storm of old school dances from different regions. Now everyone is calling the hosts to come join in. And like they knew it was their moment, with a simple look they pose. Tthen in perfect harmony, Chris in back begins the Biz Mark and Miz and Airicka follow. Then they some how transition into the Running Man. Everyone is laughing and loving it of course, smartphones and pda devices come out recording the hilarity. The three friends smile and hug once they reach the end of the line. The music is too loud to try and talk but they don't need words. This moment right here did what words could not, even after 4 years and in some cases longer.

The night quickly snowballed into a finale as time went on. Party guests began to realize that graduation and parents were waiting for them and that an even bigger party was ahead of them at Shelia's. There were those extended friends who stayed behind to help clean up. A few of the guys walked some of the ladies to their cars even though they were in a pretty safe environment, proof that chivalry was not dead. Those who couldn't make it home on their own; a dollar cab was called to get them home or they rode with someone, promising to pick up their cars in the morning. Airicka takes a few friends home of course. Miz and Chris rag on her about trying to get out of cleaning.

After the last guest leaves, Chris and Miz help one another up the stairs where they seem to crash in her room only because it was the closest. Laying on the bed they try to talk a little but seem to doze off in interchanging intervals. Chris more awake than Miz, tries to tell her about Mai. Only to be met by the soft snoring sounds of his best friend. Too tired to try and free his arm from under her, he drifts off to sleep too. They are nestled together like so many times before.
The calm of an early spring morning, subtle and quaint was the sweet

30

*tale of this city. The true pastel blue sky simmered with soft powder
like clouds and reflected the praises of the blue jays and robins.
Slowly, as the natural spotlight graces the dew of the flowers, a
paraded explosion of the biggest welcome to today, tomorrow will
never see appeared. In a small subdivision, sits a colonial style three-
bedroom home. For the past four years, this place has truly become a
sanctuary forthe three friends. Bonds have been forged over the cry of
candles. Boxes of wine have both marinated sadness and bathed a few
term papers. And there is also the aftermath of that one party that got
a little too crazy. No matter how hard you try, the memory along with
that stain in the carpet, will never be erased. Now that graduation day
has finally come, the realization that this is the last summer before the
move on has not really dawned on them. This day will be filled with so
much to do, that you may wonder if the thought will even cross their
minds. I guess we'll soon see. Whether it was partying hard till two or
three in the a.m., working late, dinner with that special someone; the
scattered remains lay lifeless unaware the shattering of morning is
about to dawn.*

*As the sun creeps through the window, the rays are halted by the
disorder of the room. Pizza boxes, half full glasses of something red as
well as a color the English language has yet to describe. A
catastrophic symphony of disarray is uniquely balanced with the harsh
presence of a peaches and crème canopy bed cater-cornered to an off
white bedroom suite. Before your eyes could avail any type of
understanding, a small clock radio blasts the revelry of today. From
underneath a Spanish twill comforter, a mellow butterscotch colored
hand swats the snooze button. Now a return to the land of solace, a
pause that is only a temporal displacement that rarely provides*

satisfaction for the body.

No sooner than you can believe, the speaker is blaring again and now the snooze button understands physical abuse. The surface changes some, as from the other side of the bed Christopher rises, yawns, and then stretches. Affirming the cluster that is mixed in the comfort of a spread and that oh so sweet spot, he simply meanders down the hall to his own room. Grabbing a towel and other morning necessities he adjourns to the bathroom outside his room. While getting into the shower he hears the sound and the throwing of an alarm clock across the room. Interjecting between the steamy raindrops...

Chris: Yo, Miz! Miz, come on girl you know we got a lot to do today! You can't be crashin' in bed all day and stuff. Yo! I swear you gonna be late fa ya own funeral. How did you get Suma Cum Laude? Miz! Yo Miz, I know you hear me, girl get up!

From the other room adjacent to the bathroom, Airicka pokes her head out of her door. Half asleep she responds as a partially dry Chris is coming out of the bathroom.

Airicka: Fa' real "C" you goin have ta chill wit the noise.

Chris: My bad shorty. But on the real you need to be up as well. I didn't think you made it home last night. You must've gotten in late. I mean did yall forget we graduate today.

Airicka: Look not everybody is on that old gotta be there right now tip.

Chris: Whatever man, you were the one shoutin from the roof the last day of class.

Airicka: Don't get mad 'cause I had the ones big enough to do it.

Chris: Yeah, when you get them from a store, of course they're big enough.

Airicka: You just mad 'cause yours ain't been unwrapped yet, Mr. Wait Till Marriage.

Chris: Why you have to go there. That's my choice. At least my girl didn't leave me for no...

Airicka: is that the best you got? An old Martin Lawrence line from a played out movie. Sad, I never thought I would live to see the day that Christopher Company would be unable to come back with the witty retort.

At the same time, a faded voice of someone squeezes from the darkness of Airicka's room, "Ki-Ki come back to bed." Chris's look shifts from chill to sautéed judgment. Even after so many years of being friends, hell "fam" her lifestyle still ruffles his feathers, truly an effect of misguided teachings. In response, she retaliates with a stern look that says more than enough to substantiate her position. The duel ends a stale mate. Emotions and looks continue to exist where bodies once stood. As Airicka's door closes back up the hall, the queen of last minute kisses the morning with harshness. Mysary, 23 years-old, runs into her bathroom. The remnants of candles free the air to absorb their

33

different tastes.

The shower steams to perfection and proceeds to burn off the whispers of the night before. Now, completely prepared to attack the morning, Miz reaches for a pair of blue cut off shorts, sports bra and her gray A.U.C. sweat top. Fully armed with keys, she shoves the money from her dresser into her pockets and she's off. Down the hall she stops in Chris's room. Leaning in the doorway, arms folded she talks to Chris who is in the closet looking for a shirt to wear.

Miz: Hey Mr. Punctuality, why are you still here?

Chris: Oh, so you got jokes? Ms. Suma Cum Lately. I got most of my stuff taken care of. Bet you can't say the same?

Miz: Loser!

Chris: Yeah, this loser got you in bed safe last night.

Miz: Okay.

Chris: No thank you? No good looking out?

Miz: We have been friends since middle school. You knew what you were getting into. Why you expecting anything from me after all this time is beyond me?

Before Chris could even respond.

Miz: You signed up for this friendship and it's a lifetime commitment. Black, Black no take back.

Chris: What!?

Miz: You heard me Black, Black no take back.

[Chris in thought] I quickly remembered that was what we both said right before we started high school when we stayed up half the night planning how we would have each others back no matter who or what came up. She always does that. It takes me back to when our friendship was so simple. I can't let her have the upper hand this time.

Chris: Yeah, but do you still have your contract?

Miz: You know I do.

Chris: Alright prove it! Go get it.

Miz: I don't need to get it. You know you signed it!

Chris: You know you can't find anything in that landslide you call a room.

Miz: Is that a challenge? Wait right here!

Chris: I'll go get the shovel.

Walking down the hall you hear Mysary shout, "Shut up!"

35

Chris: Maybe you could use Google Earth to find the floor and that would be a start.

Miz: Ooohh! I don't like you right now!
Quickly going down to her room Mysary looks in this small Victorian burgundy and gold music box that Chris gave to her for her 16th birthday. Frantically trying to remember where it was after not seeing it in the box, she hears Chris from his room.

Chris: Yo, Miz you there? Do I need to send a search party? Miz. (*Comedically making the echo noise*)

[Mysary in thought]Now you know I can't let him think don't have it. I would never hear the end of this. Of course you know this means creating verbal tactics on my part. Would I really be a true woman if I let him think he has the upper hand? And he does. This would upset the balance of female-male relations. Okay ladies, trust I got this covered. This doesn't mean you should stop prayin for me. I'm going to need all your help to pull this off. Okay here we go…

Before I could even say a word, Chris hands me this beautiful crystal 3 window picture frame. In the top frame the bazooka joe comic from our first class trip to the zoo where we got lost together and the artificially flavored treat was the bubble blowing competition that kept us calm and entertained in the Park Rangers' office. In the frame below was the date and picture of our vow of purity graduation. In the frame to the right with all the tested signs of age was my copy of the friendship contract.

Hey you? Yes you reading this, what the hell just happened? How you let me walk into this? I thought ladies look out for one another. Must be a dude reading this now.

Miz: Oh, so that whole thing was a set up? Aight you got me good this time.

Chris: Well we only graduate from college once and you might be taking that internship or that job Upstate. Literally, this is our last summer together. I thought it would be cool to give you something to remember us.

Miz: You make it sound like you won't come visit or I won't visit you.

Chris: Do you realize since 7th grade you and I have spent all of our school years and summers together?

Miz: Wow! That's a serious amount of chicken boxes.

Chris: And Sterling subs with the french fried onions. But seriously, Miz we've been though alot these past years and I just want to show you how much I really appreciate you.

The way he said it somewhat implied so much more or was it her interpretation, reading to deep into the sentiment she secretly wanted all a long. Whatever it was or was not, now a vacuum was created of any current thoughts and feelings. As if too much time had passed when it has only been a few seconds, one of them feels like "I have to say something right now".

Miz: Um um what was I saying? Oh yeah, why are you still here?

Chris: (*With a smile on the inside*) Waiting. Tischa is going to call with the information to let me know when she and Sam are on the way. Once I here from them, then I need to make a quick run to Shelia's and drop off the money. Then I need to get my line up done so I can look extra for my walk across the stage.

Miz: Ok. You sure you got time to do all that?

Chris: Well I got to do what I got to do.

Miz: Why not just say Miz, "Can you drop this off at Shelia's for me"?

Chris: I wasn't sure what you had to do before graduation.

Miz: Boy, don't play with me.

Chris: Aight then, Miz could you take this money over to Shelia's for me?

Miz: Oh so I guess I am your personal Mail carrier.

Chris: I guess it was my luck you slept late this morning huh?

Miz: It wasn't luck. G's always gotcha back. I'm just the vessel.

Chris: You right. They ain't seen the video.

Miz: They couldn't handle it if they did anyway. So what time you headed to Diamonds?

Chris: Well, Steve don't show before eleven. So I have to roll up there early if I want to be back to the house before Tischa and Sam get here.

Miz: So what time is mom coming in?

Chris: She's coming with my grandfather and they should get here around 2:30 and My sister and her family will be at the graduation around 2:00 - 2:30. She called from S.C. and said they'd be leavin' around 9:30. They didn't want me waiting on them. So Miz, what about your mom and dad? It's about a 2 hour drive right?

Miz: You know my dad, he'll leave Montgomery County at 12:30 and get here bout 12:35. We are still on for dinner Friday right?

Christopher affirms the plans, as he stands about 5'10" 195 lbs. Sorting through his clothes and finds his patchwork jean outfit. The artistry of his room is a justified balance 25 pound hand weight, an array of Forbes and Gospel Today magazines stacked neatly on his shaker table. Miz flipping through his CD collection spots a brand new fitted cap on the dresser.

Miz: Hey, let me borrow this? Thanks.

Chris: If I would've said no, you would've just taken it anyway right?

Miz: You're right. Well I'm out, hitcha' lata.

Chris: You on your way to meet up with Deneese (Neecie)?

Miz: What you trying to say? The do don't look tight?

Chris: There you go with that. I thought yall were doing the girl thing today. Didn't you tell me there was something y'all were doing for her to get her shop up and running?

Miz: That's right clean it up. Nah, we took care of that yesterday.

Chris is clearly fishing for what she has planned. Miz still reluctant to relay her actual plans with Darik, so responds with a calculated answer that will be truthful.

Miz: I got to run out and do a few things. You know I am helping with the wedding plans, then an early brunch...

Christopher is looking at her as if to ask another question, but the bitter kiss of reservation invades his conscious. Like clock work, a good morning text vibrates his hip from a new number.

Miz: Who's that?

How do you answer this question without opening a can of worms in a short span of time? You can't lie, this is clearly not the time to talk about this. Just then a second message come through.

Chris: Just another congratulations.

To be honest it has never been this hard to tell Mysary about a new woman. Why is this one different? He just met her yesterday. He wants to talk but the words won't come out. I mean, she has Darik right? So it should be simple, easy as a piece of cake? Recognizing that there is something there, she asks...

Miz: What up?

Quickly changing his posture wiping clear traces of what he wants to talk about and at the same time never forgetting she is with Darik and that won't change, especially with the Onyx chain around her neck.

Christopher: Nothing, just ... neva mind.

Mysary: A' ight, i'm out.

Mysary walks out the door leaving Christopher looking at the place where she once stood. The emotional jet wash traps him in a daze. Airicka geared up for her morning pre-graduation duties opens her door to see Chris in his room sitting on the edge of the bed. The relationship between Airicka and Christopher is strange, his religious upbringing often clashes with her personal lifestyle but in the four years, they have really been in one another's corner more than you could imagine. She never tried to hide or boast about who she was and he never acted so super spiritual around her. Some would venture to believe that Mysary was the common bond between the two of them. But in 4 years, they were able to put differences aside pretty quickly and manage to have some truly defining moments that only Christopher and Airicka can explain. It is a friendship to the fullest extent of the

41

word, no doubt. So I guess you could say it is not all that strange. Most friendships start from a strange or wild encounter. With that, she stops at his room before she goes off.

Airicka: You a'ight? Yo C you a'ight man?

Christopher: ... Huh? yeah everything's cool.

Airicka: I heard Miz and you talking. You gave her the picture frame right?

Christopher: Yeah

Airicka: So, you ever gonna say somethin?

Christopher: What?

Airicka: Dude, It's been 4½ almost 5 years that I have known the two of you. You still haven't said anything to her. I mean its obvious you got feelings for her. You just need to say something . C'mon with everything that she told me the two of you have been through as friends, you don't think about you and her and not her and him. If I were you I would...

Clearly frustrated about the insinuations, Chris brushes off the attempt with a quick look and even quicker comment.

Christopher: But ya ain't me, so whatchu yappin about?

42

Airicka: Miz is my girl and I thought we were tight also. To tell the truth, you're playin' yourself by not saying what you feel. My dad once told me, if you want something bad enough, nothing should stop you.

When faced with the truth about our feeling we get defensive, why is that? Christopher never lets on that he wants to loose his cool. I mean she is right, he does think about making that move. But how do you tell your friend of 17 years, to dump her dude and get with you? This ain't the movies. Besides that, what is this new feeling for Mai anyway? Airicka's assault of truth continues.

Airicka: She still doesn't know about what you did sophmore year for her does she?

Christopher: And she won't find out will she? (*Raising one eyebrow to express the true emotional intent of his statement.*) So what are you sayin' and why do you care?

Airicka: Look dude I didn't come to argue. I was just showin' a little concern. I promised you I wouldn't tell so I won't. Besides, that is something she should know when the time is right. It's better if it came from you anyway.

Christopher: Well, this is not the time.

Airicka: I will be back in a about an hour. I talked to Tischa, she said they will be here at 1:45 to pick us up. She said she would call you back.

Christopher realizing no real need to be snappy at Airicka, she has always been outspoken and to some degree she is right.

Christopher: Yo, my bad for getting all testy.

Airicka: No prob. Just remember two to the nose (*Thumbing her nose like a fighter*).

Christopher:…Means one to the chin.

And just that quickly everything is dissolved

Airicka: Renee will be out in a few minutes, she's going to take a shower. A'ight then, Peace.

Throwing up two fingers walking down the stairs spitting words of Langston Hughes; Airicka is out the door. Just as it closes the phone rings. Christopher and Tischa talk for a bit. He informs her that Miz was going to drop the money off and that the next practice will be at Sheila's. The ocassional quick joke about finally being done with school and how hard it will be to get in the routine of normal life is shared.

Somewhere in that time Renee jumps into the shower. Chris recognizing now he has to wait until she is ready to leave before he can bounce, still on the phone with Tischa he checks the time. Exhaling his emotion, T inquires whats going on. It's not the gentlemen nor the fact that men don't gossip, Chris just doesn't really talk about what's bothering him to his female friends.

44

Yeah the surface feeling conversations are normal but the real heart to heart stuff is reserved for a select few. So T gets the normal brush off "It's nothing" Dressed in some of Airicka's clothes Renee, last nights clothes in hand looks into the Chris's room to see if he was able to walk her to the door. Phone still in hand he says very little but respectfully walks with her. Opening the door, Renee leaves turning to wave goodbye Chris nods. Looking at the clock, Chris realizes he has to get to the barbershop before it fills up so he grabs his bag tells Tischa later and rolls out the house too.

It's now a little after 11:00, Mysary is pulling up to Gampy's. Checking her looks in the mirror, she parks and enters the restaurant. The soft breeze of jazz plays across the room, not too many people are eating yet. The hostess ask how many in the party. Before she could respond, Darik comes from the other side...

Derik: She with me. Thank you. (*This being the code he discussed earlier.*) Hey Sweetie, we are over here. Wow! Man your hair smells great.

Mysary: Only you.

Derik: What?

Mysary: Nothing... Not it looks good but it smells good. You are crazy.

Derik: I took the liberty of ordering your favorite, Strawberry Lemonade.

Mysary: Thanks, sorry i'm late.

Derik: Hey, the world doesn't need another sorry woman.

Mysary: Anyway, as I was saying before I was so rudely interrupted, I apologize for being so late.

Derik: Don't worry about it, the wait is cool. I mean I understand with this being graduation day and all, some things are going to jump off. You are here now. So you ready?

Mysary: You know me, right?

Derik: Why do you think I asked? Is there something I can help with?

Mysary: I got to run this one solo.

Derik: Well, although you run solo; know this, you are not alone.

[Mysary in thought] Okay, let me explain something, my life just like my room may often look like a masterpiece of confusion but I know where things are because I put them there. Growing up I chose to set my own path. I would not fall into any type cast of what a preacher's daughter should be. First thing, we are not all freaks. Some of us hold tight to certain things if you know what I mean. I had to be different. As early as Kindergarten I made sure I was the best, but not for recognition sake just because I could. It became the driving force that is me. Be the best and no one can tell you what to do. Teachers, coaches, all luv'd me everywhere I went I made the name Mysary mean

46

something. Never with the big head because the true friends I had would always keep me grounded, especially my "[2]G". Me and "G", oh "G" and I, excuse me, well we got a special type of relationship going on, always clownin' me and that is really all I can say about that.

Well when it came time for interaction with others I never depended on the praise of people. I was my own cheering section. I guess that is why guys seemed to be intimidated by me in school. You know? Champion of the Math and Debate team; Anchor on the swim team and a host of other things. I had a lot of male friends most of whom were older than me and they treated me like a little sister. Yeah on the come up, I know some of them had other thoughts but they played it cool. One friend remained constant, Chris. We never tried the boyfriend-girlfriend thing, he was just Chris and I was me. Not saying I haven't thought about it or us, but I refuse to put myself out there without knowing how he feels.

Truthfully speaking, I will always love him. I bet when we're old and he calls me from the home, I will be there. That's just the way it has been. I can count on him and he can count on me.

You know how it is when your girl is trippin'? You call that friend to make it plain to you what the hell you did or didn't do. Yeah, you think you know Chris, but I know the real Christopher J. Company, and I have to tell you, he has had his moments like every guy has had with relationships. I tried to keep my distance because you know we women

---

[2] G is short for GOD switching around me and G to G and I just means putting God first.

are territorial. No matter what I did to avoid them or stay clear of their thing, his women always got the green eyes when they met me even when we double dated. Like any true friend he saw me through some tough times. He always pushed me beyond what I saw in me. As fickle as I was, he could see past that and get to the real me even if I wasn't sure who I was at the time. After this serious relationship with Bryan ended kind of messy, I went on this internal tangent not really sure what I wanted. Like clock work, Christopher was there to be a friend and help me get me together. It wasn't some accidental kiss or screw in a moment of weakness that brought us together, just friendship. I mean who does that?

So maybe a year after the Bryan fiasco, and I know you maybe wondering who the hell is Bryan? In a nut shell I liked him, he kinda wanted a piece of me. I could say I was young, stupid, crazy in like with him. So I lied to my parents about who I was seeing and snuck out many a nights to be with him, well drive him home from the bar where he worked and got drunk. I was 17 he was 24 with two baby mommas that I knew of. Well you can see why I was into him. Yeah like you don't have a ticket stub from psycho land. Continuing on, there was this one time we had gone out to dinner and before we could get our food, this pregnant woman with a little one in her arms came out of nowhere and started in on him. Calling him a lazy no count so and so and she was going to kick my ass. You can imagine this was the wake up call I needed to get out of this mess. I am giving you the Cliff Notes version because to tell you the story is another book entirely. Ok, so here is where Chris comes in, on my way home I not only catch a flat, I was on one of the darkest roads ever. We talkin' blacker than a trillion midnights black. You already know I couldn't call my parents for obvious reasons. It had to be about 9 or 9:30. I had $12 in my pocket when I called Chris. He didn't ask what happened, he simply said, "What you need shorty?" I was ready to cry. I didn't know what he was able to do, seeing as how he didn't have a car. He asked me where I was, snuck out of the house, and road his bike 3 miles with a flashlight taped to the handlebars. He changed my tire and all the way home he never once said I told you so. How we never got caught sneaking in and out of the house is still amazing. Bryan continued to call for a few weeks and somehow his baby momma got my number. I never answered the phone again when I saw a number that even had the faintest hint of his number I just rejected it. Chris has really bailed me out of some wild situations.

Anywho as I was saying, one summer while on my way to CPR training, I met Derik. He made me laugh the entire time. Being that we were the youngest two in the class by maybe 15 - 20 years it seemed. Derik and I started talking after class and exchanged numbers. He never rushed the, "I luv you" line. He was happy just kickin it. We never made the agreement to be exclusive, it was just understood. What I liked most about him was his respect of my vow of purity. Hell yes, sometimes I want to take this ring off and hurl it into the river and get it on but it's not that easy. There is too much at stake. I mean if the relationship is good without sex then why add the drama and pressure? Understandably, Derik has been pretty good with keeping things safe. The first year was really rough though. Can I tell you there were a lot of fricken prayers, cold showers, and contemplations? Somehow, Shit! Who am I kidding it was all GOD that was in total control. The best part is when G would look at me and say "I Love You in spite of you". With all that said, Derik and I just grew together not really sure how or

49

when it happened it just did. So here we are going on three and a half years and it has been a ride. I know it's been hard on him. Hmm, maybe after graduation we could... what am I saying? Look at him sitting there looking so fine um, um, um!

Derik: Hey what are you thinking about?

Myasary: Nothing. Why do I look like I have something on my mind?

Derik: Nah, That's just it. You seem to be pretty level for all you got going on. Not to mention the smile on your face. What? You been dippin in the communion wine again?

Mysary: Don't you see the "S"? It's tatted there for a reason.

Derik: Here we go again. (*uttering the music of Voltron as if it's background theme to a long winded speech*).

Mysary: Oh you got jokes? You heathen.

Derik: Yo I know Jesus.

Mysary: Last I checked, it took more than saying God bless you to be saved.

Derik: Whatever man.

The waiter approaches from behind Mysary with a covered silver tray in hand. Sensing his presence, she turns. Not one to really show the

50

outward emotion, a soft smile fades to her lips. Looking at Derik as if to say what have you gone and done this time. His reply is equally as silent but filled with his signature smirk. After the cover is lifted there is revealed a small box and a card size envelope. Taking both of course, she opens the card first. A hand written message on the outside says "Billions have no clue, millions try to make it, thousands even hundreds fake it, looking over the years I realize it all comes down to me and you".

Mysary: (*reading the inside of the card a loud*) I knew you would read this first so here it goes. Every moment is like that first day in June. From that look, to an embrace, and down to the second with you means…[open the box now].

After opening the box, a small globe bridled in gold is covered with purple tissue paper.

[Mysary] Sometimes he can be really amazing. He says that for all that I have done for him he just wanted to give me the world. I mean come on you have to admit, that takes skill.

Now is one of those rare occasions where the secret emotions of the bat cave are reared in the form of a kiss initiated by Miz. Yes the master of stoicism does have a softer side. The challenge of touching this part is not even a quarter as gratifying as the fruit of such labor. The slow soft withdrawal of her honey buttered lips places Derik in some type of passionate paralysis.

Derik: Yo, next time you plan to kiss me like that, please give me a running jump or something.

Miz: Don't ruin the moment.

Derik: Nah, babe I mean well…

Miz: Just let it go.

Derik nods at the waiter to bring the bill. After one glance he slides his card in and places it on the edge of the table. Miz takes a look at the check and before placing it down says…

Miz: I'm expensive aren't I?

Derik: Never that.

Miz: Yes I am. You ain't got to deny it. Certain things you just learn to accept about yourself. My daddy made sure we had everything we needed. His thought was he never wanted a dude to use provision as means of gaining access. You add that to my already strong-minded belief system and you got yourself a pretty pricey woman on your hands.

Derik: If I say you are expensive then I am not qualified to be with you. Expensive is saying you are beyond my means of acquisition. You know I don't play that.

Miz: A'ight then (with a smile) Big brotha Almigh-TEE.

Derik: Get out of my head, man. As soon as I said that, I started thinking about that movie.

Now the bill is paid and the two talk for a few more minutes before leaving. Walking her to her car, Derik fights within. He wants to hold her hand but he recounts the many subtle but strong arguments against public displays of affection. How something so small could weigh so heavy on someone with relationship insecurities. No guy is comfortable with his woman being friends with another man gay or not. Especially the NOT gay ones. Ever since Miz and Derik got together, he has felt like his place is second fiddle. Now, Derik doesn't have the artistic means of expression nor does he share in the precious bond that unites Christopher and Mysary. Constantly tormented by thoughts Derik engages in this battle by performing tasks to compensate for what he feels is missing. When arguments arise even after 2 1/2 years, he still questions why she chose him. Comparing the level of closeness and trying to figure why he is on the short end of the stick.

Miz: Thank you for lunch and everything. (*Mysary leans in for a kiss. This is a very uncommon guesture. Derik oblivious to the fact continues talking*)

Derik: My pleasure. (*Now standing in front of her car*) Well I know you gotta jet, so see you at 3:00.

Miz: That's it?

Derik: What?

Miz: Oh I try to be affectionate and all I get is see you at 3?

Derik: Nah, never that...

Before he could rant Miz grabs his hand and slowly caresses the small of his head and neck. Looking up with those cinnamon eyes and sweet ebony lips she begins a two-lip butterfly. At first, the shock flutters his heart to the point of exhaustion. Quick to recover, now his hands are around the small of her waist and the embrace is like a gentle blend of satin whispers fainting on a field of lilies. With no words they go their separate ways with gentle smiles and looks that bid a fond adu...

Now on the expressway flying to pick up her dress from the tailors, still listening to her pastor speak on relationships. The words kind of repel off of her as her attention is focused on the objective ahead and the list of tasks to do before the she has to go to the Woodruff Arts Center.

Back at home, Chris and Airicka are waiting on Tischa and Sam, they all agreed to ride together in one car. Chris's mom called and asked for directions to the Hall because she made a wrong turn somewhere. There was construction going on and traffic was being redirected.

Airicka: Everything alright?

Chris: Yeah man, Moms going to meet us at the Hall. The roads are all jacked up.

Airicka: How long she going to be here again? I just want to know if she'll make her famous veggie patties and coco bread.

Chris: I made sure she hit up Sterlings, New York Trollies, and the Bodega on North and Covington. She said she was brining all the good stuff. You know what that means?

Airicka & Chris: Almond Smash!

They spend a glorious moment thinking back on the different visits and the goodies she brought over the years, and how extra delicious her veggie patties and coco bread are. No matter how many times they tried they could never come close to what she did. Then, the moment was shattered by the beep of the horn and the simultaneous ringing of the doorbell. Airicka opening the door to a dancing Tischa...

Airicka: Hey T.

Tischa: Hey girl! I gotta go and you know how Sam is.
Going upstairs with the quickness. The phone rings and Chris answers with thought that it is Miz calling needing something.

Chris: Talk to me.

Changing tone with the recognition of Mai's voice.

Chris: Hey you?

Mai: Just calling to wish you the best on graduation day. I know you are probably on your way out the door. I was thinking I would really like to finish our conversation from yesterday but I never got your address. I was taking a chance that you would be home. I mean with all you got going on and everything. I'm not being too impetuous am I?

Chris: Yo, that's bananas. I was just thinking about you and you called.

Mai: Fa' Real. I must have done some real work on you if you thinking bout little old me on graduation day and all. So, what were you thinking about?

They converse like they've known each other for a while. No apparent inhibitions or reservations they just flow off one another. Diverting attention away from the question, Chris informs Mai the new venue for the after party is Shelia's Café'. Catching a glimpse of Tischa coming down the stairs he realizes once again the timing is terrible. Both of them do not want to end the short lived verbal dance. Mai is first to make the disconnection. Isn't it amazing that even after so many years the cat and mouse game is still affective? No matter how smart you think you are, somehow you still get caught in its trap. One would guess that the disguise of friendly flirtation clouds the mind and lulls it to sleep.

Sam has beeped "the hurry your tail" tune more than once. Chris ends the conversation at the same time as Airicka and Tischa converge at the bottom of the stairs.

Airicka: Hey, who was that on the phone?

Before he could respond Tischa requires some affirmation.

56

Tischa: Hey girl, how is my hair?

Now Sam beeps the horn in that tune "one last time". How is it that the horn of a car could really give off the emotion of a person? So they all leave before any mayhem gets started. Airicka affirms the style as Chris holds the door open for them. As they rush to the car, Chris locks the door and dawns his cap and jumps in the back seat.

Sam: We ready now?

Airicka: Uncle Sam are we there yet?

Gently caressing his knee. Tischa tries to soften the mood as they leave the driveway. Airicka and Chris play the role of children on a long journey bum rushing Tischa and Sam with the typical, "Mommy, he hit me", "Daddy, I gotta go pottie!". You can always count on your friends to make a pressure situation fun. Reaching the symphony hall, at the same time as many others, you see people fixing, primping and rushing. Exhaling, they all get out of the car and make their way in with the occasional crazy group pose for that picture to commemorate each moment. In between the straddle hush of nerve and breath the majestic tapestry swelled with anticipation as the graduates stood in the Hall. Some arriving in groves while others scramble in half dressed, cap in mouth looking to find where they're to be placed. Even after four years of late night cross breed cram sessions once you found where you were supposed to stand in line, 85% fall victim to CGS (Click Gravity Syndrome). The Lead Coordinator is now going up and down the line looking for any missing candidates as well as trying to maintain order, like that would ever happen. As honors are being handed out, the door opens for some of those who did not receive to conjure up tales of why they were denied as if the space between 3.3 and 3.8 is minimal. Small cells of conversation grow to a dull roar and spawn other conversations to the point clapping voices is the new silence. Annoyed by everyone, the Lead Coordinator silences the crowd.

Coordinator: LeNoir? My-Sary LeNoir? Is there a My-sar-ee Lay No-r here?

Wendall: Yo man, where ya girl at?

Christopher: Dude you know the routine. You're the one to talk. I don't see Rae nowhere. What up wit that? Yo, who you think gonna be here first?

Wendall: Really though? They have to be related or something. Bananas! All I can say is bananas! How two of the top graduates gonna be late? Now you know I can't bet against my girl and have her find out.

Christopher: Oh, did you and Rae decide on what you're going to do?

Wendall: Yeah, it took some work, but she saw my side. This decision didn't come easy either. You know I had to make her feel it was safe and secure to do this. Even after two and a half years she is still waiting for that other shoe to drop. Check this out.
Pulling from his pocket a soft crème colored velvet Tiffany's case to show an impressive half ct. Princess cut blue diamond engagement

ring. Surely this draws a lot of attention. So then questions begin to swirl. Caught up in the attention, the surprise is almost foiled when Mysary and Raven both come in the group just as Wendall puts the ring back in his pocket.

Mysary: So what y'all taking about? Let me guess, outside bets on who would get here first?

Raven: They wouldn't. Right sweetie?

Wendall: Nah, never that bae. You know how we do, guys talk.

Mysary: Right.

Chris: Yo Miz, I need to talk to you about something.

Miz: Whas up?

And of course before they could get into anything serious, the orchestra began to play and it was time to enter the auditorium. Mysary is being pulled to her perspective place in line. Being found by the coordinator, she is swarmed by an entourage of instructions.

Now normally the graduation sequence would be a simple transition into the next series of events. As you probably can already, tell this situation is far from normal. Wendall and Raven, we'll save that for some other time. Trust they will show up again, I promise. As the candidates walk down the aisle, cameras flash as howls, hoots and whoofs tango with the processional. Mysary and Raven share the honor of being this year's Suma Cum Laude. Theirs is a convenient friendship. They don't need to talk much to validate the bond, but when they do come together it is almost like the conversation never ended. Mysary making sure to eye her confidant Airicka; who managed to graduate with a 3.75 while holding down two jobs and taking care of some knotted family affairs.

Airicka many times wanted to drop out not because of pressure and definitely not money, but she felt like the people were just too fake. Also the constant misuse and mental abuse from those who didn't even know her gave her moments where "Fuck it" just seemed to be the best option. I guess that's why she stayed close to Mysary. They balanced an approach that kept the haters at bay. Mysary was chosen to give the commencement address. This is one of those times where the words speak for themselves, but in order for them to become life changing meaningful expansions of breath, she will need the love and confidence of her inner circle. Briefly looking at Christopher, Airicka and clutching the hand of Raven, they all seemed to feel that a friend is in need. Each one possesses a different aspect that helps Miz to stand, openly drawing from them is not the norm but as i said before, this is not a normal situation. Now not in its entirety but here it is...

Mysary: George Bernard Shaw said, "I like a state of continually becoming, with a goal in front, not behind." 10 years from now you will arrive, the question is, where will you be? Today, this afternoon, right now, I would like to upset your thinking so that when this moment is over you won't fall victim to the thief who goes by the name of procrastination. It's time to get motivated! It's time to get smart and its time to get moving! Procrastination decreases options. The longer you wait, the fewer choices you have. Now is the time to correct the next

10 years...

Four years ago, we were a bunch of thoughts, drawn to this campus for whatever reason. Some raced in at breakneck speed keeping with family tradition and others were just a brain fart away from getting the U-Haul and returning home. We all started with these big ideas, these "wisions" wishful visions of being and becoming only to be given a crash course in reality. What we see is a lie. It's true. How many times have you looked in the mirror and your left hand is on the right side? I tell you this, you can't always believe everything you see. I remember at Orientation, someone saying look to your left and look to your right, the person you see won't be here next year. And from those late night runs to Kinkos at 32¢ per minute to those Ramen Noodle casserole potlucks during finals, no matter the obstacle we faced we are all here having made the trek. So now that we've made it, where are we? Better yet, who are we?....

A professor once said, "Procrastination decreases your options." It's true the more time you spend being inactive, the more opportunity flies by you. Well everything, but those loans we have to pay back. If we are to fix the next 10 years, then we must get smart. We must get going and get active. Assess what you have and work it to the fullest. You do what you do because you believe what you believe. If you believe nothing good will ever happen. Why are you surprised when only bad things happen? So many of us had no idea we would graduate, let alone choose the careers we chose. I bet you everyone sitting here knows, we have to work what we got before our parents or Sallie Mae comes calling. Look, your words are what create the environment you live in. Quite a few people say they want an above average job with an above average salary. The problem with this statement is that it is only made by a below average thinker. If you want above average you have to be above average.

...There needs to be measurable progress in reasonable time or else some substantial changes need to be made. Everything in life has a purpose, meaning it serves a function or job. This is not an attempt to quantify or qualify your existence by the things you do. So I ask again, 10 years from now you will arrive and the question remains, where will you be? As we chase cars, jobs, or hunt whatever will define our journey, examine your motives but more importantly consider how much time you are willing to put in. Reasonable time is a simple ratio of thought to accomplishment. For every thought there should be an equal or greater accomplishment that follows.

(*Looking out into the crowd holding her left hand up with thumb pinched against two fingers*) This is thought. (*Now holding up her right hand in the same manner but at a distinct distance opposite the left*) This is accomplishment. The bridge between the two is discipline. You want to be a better whatever you are then don't just think it, you must discipline yourself to the point of achieving the goal of your thought. Now that you know, you have to say to yourself I must get active. I must get educated, and I must get...

...going. No seriously I must get going because my time with you is over. Thank you.

At the conclusion of her speech, a large roar of applause floods the air. Wendall, and Raven all clown asking those around to pass their offerings forward and asking is there anyone that needs salvation.

Christopher looking from the crowd directly connecting with her notices how nervous she is. He smiles that calming smile stating a job well done. She rests in that her best friend and her man are both there to support her. Derik nods to that modern laid back tempo of that's me up there, if you know what I mean.

Quite a few are moved by her words and others are stuck in awe. The President and other school delegates stand and prepare to give degrees to the candidates. Now what is important about this moment is that when Christopher comes to the stage he looks to see his people cheering big time. Smiling in their direction in the back of the auditorium he spots a face that for a moment stuns him. Almost falling down the steps, Mai looks at him with a warm smile of hello. Coming out of his mini coma, he returns to his seat not focused on the Bachelors degree he just received but looking back from time to time in disbelief. Unable to stay, she mouths that she has to go back to work and she will see him later. Responding a pretend cry and with a thank you for coming, she tips out the back. By this time, Wendall is back to his seat and he is trying to figure out who or what Chris was talking to. Clowning as usual...

Wendall: Yo I know you don't think somethin' bout to jump off up in here. Earth to Chris? Man I been wantin' ta tell you something for a long time...

Chris: What?...

Wendall: I love you man.

Chris: What?

Wendall: Do they speak English in what? (*after a moment of serious laughter*) I ain't never seen you at a loss for words, son.

Chris: Yo Wen, when I tell you yesterday I met this shorty at the park. I'm thinking, we'll hook up tonight at Sheila's, you know get the chance to talk. On the real, I sware I just saw her.

Wendall: She pop up just to see a brotha graduate? Yeah, so where is she at?

Chris: (*Looking around unable to spot her.*) She had to go back to work I guess. I mean, she was back there.

Wendall: Right. Yo fa' real son, you sure she ain't got you twisted and she stalking you or something? Don't get no bricks thrown through your window at 3 in the morning.

Chris: Why you gotta bring that up? See that's why I don't tell you stuff you always gotta bring the past. Oh but I guess it's all cool when some people start trippin' ain't that right "Willey Lump lump"...

Wendall: Don't go there...

Chris: (*singing*) It's so hooooot! I'm burning up. What have I just stuck my thing in?...

Calling a mutual truce before the closets are cleaned out, they show support for other members of the graduating class. Conversations float now as people are preparing to go and get their grubb on and of course confirming the new venue for the after party. While some stare at each intricate design of their degree as if they can't believe it really belongs to them. Occasionally, there is the person walking across the stage to the uproar of friends and family. As nicknames are shouted out from classmates and special interest clicks, the energy is now rising as they get closer and closer to the end. A few of the Deltas are armed with sorority colored confetti guns. The swelling of excitement has now filtered into the audience. Cameras are set, video cameras and camera phones are checked for approximate battery life. Now the last person Zibiddiah Zwick has received his degree and before the closing caps go flying, kisses are shared confetti guns are on blast and other congratulatory exchanges are given.

The after-graduation festivities include hugs and kisses from family, friends and partners. Shouts of "it's over!" and "hallelujah I did it!" ring out in the vestibule of the symphony hall. Of course, before people can go out and eat they have to pose for pictures. Video cameras, cell phones and other digital devices flash, click, and record the personal celebrations. And you know once the Kappas start, the Q's and Alpha's aren't far behind. This time the battle lines are down and it's all about the joy and honor. There is a spirit of togetherness that is seen at celebratory functions that withers racial and social barriers. If this could only be bottled and everyday be a celebration what would become of us? I digress. Catching up with their folks and each other Chris, Miz, Sam, Tischa and Airicka all hug and share their joy. Of course dinner celebrations are all over town with five schools graduating the same day. Sitting in the restaurant you can't help but look at all the different colors of caps and gowns, balloons, flowers, cards etc. A lot of laughter and smiles feed the air as friends and family all become one. There was even a wedding proposal and all eyes were on this when the sound of amazement shattered the clanking of glasses and overshadowed laughter. About two to three hours later and after everything on the menu has been eaten, except thank you please come again, most people are leaving while the next group of patrons are coming in.

Now is the time to ditch the folks and get the party started. Sheila's Café is a local spot familiar to all the college heads and the art community. It was started as an off campus spot where you could get some of the best falafel or pastries this side of your momma's kitchen. In addition, it has become the exposure capitol for some great local talent. With every new hour, more people come in many still wearing their caps and tassels. The cheers and ovations get louder as this two story café' begins to fill up. MYSTC radio station D.J. Spyn Doctor is non stop with the hype jams and mixing in a few classics. As soon as the floor looks likes it is thinning out, he do that infamous scratch hold up wait a minute and whatever comes on you better believe the floor fills back up.

Miz, Airicka, and Chris are all jamming together on the floor starting the soul train party line. The noise level is really too high to talk so it's just that follow my lead type of thing. Tischa and Sam join in the fun by steping. Being that Spyn Doctor is from Chicago, without missing a beat he drops this sweet tune and the dance floor shifts to a steppers ball with more than half the place sporting their moves and the others trying to learn. Some take this opportunity to relax a little or at least

66

get something to drink. The atmosphere is right for conversation.

They are like the three amigos when they enter a place. With Chris, Miz, and Airicka having so many different connections, acquaintances and friends walking through the crowd to even find a table is fun. They take turns pulling the other two away from picture moments and hugs. The 5-minute journey feels like a lifetime expedition. Finally they're here at the table and before they could get comfortable it's like the seats spring them in all different directions but there is that moment as the group huddle to establish who is getting the libation and who gets the vitals...

Chris: Yo, what yall want from the bar?

Airicka: Blue Magic.

Miz: Day at the Beach.

Chris: You pick me up some of those [3]Rockefeller Mushrooms Sheila says they are the bomb?

Airicka: Ooh, where they at?

Chris: Over by the raw bar.

Airicka: Miz you want something?

---

[3] Recipe: Rockafella Mushrooms (p.288)

Miz: Not right now.

Airicka: Okay I'll bring you some of the [4]Bang Bang Shrimp back.

Miz: Good girl, cause you know I would hurt you if ya didn't. I will hold down the table until you guys comeback.

Airicka & Chris: Right!

Miz: What's that s'pposed to mean?

Airicka: It won't be long

Miz: Long for what?

Chris: Before you go on the floor shakin' your ass.

Miz: Y'all know me. it ain't like that.

Chris: Exacts! We know you all too well.

Airicka: Just make sure nobody snags our seats okay?

Miz: Whatever! I got this.

Just then "It takes Two" comes on in the DJ's mix and almost like a bolt of lightening Mysary is about to crash the floor. Like the weight of

---

[4] Recipe: Bang Bang Shrimp (p.290)

four eyes look, not in amazement but like really? that has to be a new record. Rather than hit the dance floor though, she stands at the edge of the table looking back at Chris and Airicka like "I told you, I got this" So they disband for the moment to complete their quest. Mysary, holds down the table but still gets her groove on. From behind, a hand first, then a body draws very close as lips pollinate the right ear with sweet whispers.

Derik: Have i told you how beautiful you are to me? Please, if I may, (*extending his hand to her*) come away with me.
The bass caressed with the strength of a million secret fantasies embraced all at once and the gentleness of babies breath brushing against a field of roses. Eyes twitching teeth unable to create even the most coherent chatter, she feels the aroma of her man swell around her. Within a matter of seconds she can never let on that she was affected by this in any way. Mysary quickly regains her composer and smiles to say.

Miz: You better kiss me quick before my man comes and I change my mind.

Turning around quickly looking sarcastically shocked.

Miz: Oh Derik when did you get here?

All his insecurities flood in a second and recede even quicker with that look. I want him to command what is his and enjoy the bounty waiting. SeeIi knew he needed me to want him with my statement looming heavy, he had to have reassurance that my affection was there from the moment I heard him. His kiss though small, breathes through me, He knows when to talk to me, hug me, and his touch is the perfect blend of appreciation and security. If you could only feel him you would know what I mean, but don't get any ideas he is mine.

At the same time of this momentary affair with time and space Christopher and Airicka return to the table goodies in hand. The music is in total control of Airicka even in a waiting stance she moves to the rhythm. Finally the music fades for a few announcements, this gives room for some conversation..

Derik: What up B?

Christopher: You got it. A "[5]Day at the Beach" and a "Blue Magic"

Derik: Looks like the party is right here. Yo, what's a Blue Magic?

Airika: Armadale, Blue something and a Sour something.

Derik: I'm afraid to find out what's in this.

Mysary: Chris, Who was behind the bar, Donte' or Rick?

Christopher: They both were. Donte' made these.

Airicka & Mysary: Oh yeah! (*Laughing seriously at their unison review*)

---

[5] Recipe: Blue Magic (p.295) Day at the Beach (p.295)

Derik: Am I missing something here?

Mysary: Take a sip.

Derik: Whoa! That's hot right there! What's in it?

Mysary: Grey Goose, Peach Schnapps, and a bunch of other stuff.

Derik: For real? How did you deal with these two?

With their eyes zeroed in the only safe response was none.

Derik: Aw, come on dude it's not like that is it?

Airicka & Mysary: WELL IS IT?

Although this is a joking moment, the understanding is self-preservation is a must. Even at the expense of a fellow soldier sometimes. The opening is there, she always presents herself at the right time. Misdirection is the only ally that can open a doorway of escape.

Christopher: Like what? I don't know what you are talking about. Maybe you can explain it?

Mysary: Yeah, Like what?

Once all focus is taken off Christopher now, he is free to make a prompt exit. Hanging around can only lead to your downfall. Christopher makes a dart to the bathroom eluding detection and

71

leaving Derik to fend for himself. Spending a few extra moments in the restroom, Christopher feels the air should be clear. Coming out, Donte' the bartender calls Chris over, asking about Airicka's current relationship status and if he would put in a good word.

Before returning to the table he spots Mai as she comes in the door down stairs. He is making every effort not to lose sight of her before reaching her. Of course, trying to yell her name would not be advised. Not because any remaining cool points would be eliminated but the current volume would put a tremendous strain on his vocal chords. With less than 10 ft. between them she can see him making his way toward her. Now face to face, smiles embrace in a feverish excitement uncontained.

Chris: Hey, glad you made it!

Mai: Figured since I was on your mind and all, I might as well pay you a visit. Wow, is the entire graduating class here?

Chris: You know how it is when you say party, everybody and their grandmother shows up. Would you like something to drink?

Mai: What would you suggest?

Chris: [6]The Cape Cod Tea is off the charts.

Mai: Sounds good. Is there somewhere a little less crowded?

------

[6] Recipe: Cape Cod Tea (p.296) Poop in the Water (p. 296)

Chris: Sure. Just let me get our drinks. Donte', yo Donte' two Cape Cod Teas.

Donte': Bet!

Chris: So what new creations have you come up with?

Donte': You wanting to try something?

Chris: Not this go-round, but what you working on?

Donte': Dude I got this killer shot and a drink I made by accident. They are the bomb, son. The shot I like to call Poop in the Water and the other is [7]I Can Drink Some Shit.

Chris: Bananas, dude strictly bananas. I'll be sure to tell my roomies.

Donte': Do that!

Stepping to the bar a few seconds after the order was placed is Brevin; comedian and friends with Airicka with a special emphasis on the friend part. Now, he is not her luv interest because a woman like Airicka is never interested in luv, or so it would seem. They kick it from time to time sometimes crossing over into their separate relationships but it is what it is.

Brevin: Yo son what up?

---

[7] I Can Drink Some Shit recipe (p.296)

Chris: B-Real! (*slapping a pound*) what is up fam?

Brevin: Trying to make a dollar out of 15¢.

Chris: You ready for the show?

Brevin: The real question is, are they ready for me? I have been working on some new stuff that is sure to kill.

Chris: I hear that. Airicka is up stairs with Miz.

Brevin: Tha's wha's up. Good looking out.

Chris: No problem.

Donte': Two Cape Cod Coolers. Here you go.

Chris: Thanks. (*Turning his attention to Brevin before grabbing the drinks*) Yo B, I'm out. We'll hook up later in the week and talk more about the show. You planning to be by the spot this week?

Brevin: You know how that is?

Chris: Holla.

Grabbing the drinks Christopher leads the way to the patio where although there are many people outside the volume is committed to more intimate conversation. Each table is draped in salmon and rose colored cloth with a lemon-honey scented candle centered in a curved hand blown vase. The dim lights and the cover of night blend with the caressing breeze to create a mood that could only be described as awesome.

Chris: How is this (*Suggesting one of the corner tables*)

Mai: This is nice.

After placing the drinks on the table he pulls out her chair, they both sit. For a moment or two aimless stares are broken up when their eyes connect. This is that first time stuff when you have so much to say but you don't know what to say first. So they try to talk, at the same time of course by accident, both defer to the other to the point smiles seem to be the only form of consistent conversation.

Mai: I have an idea. We each take a minute and give only facts about ourselves.

Chris: I'm with that.

Mai: I'll start. I'm 24 years old. I'm 5'6. I don't smoke. I do however favor a nice Chianti every once in a while. I'm single. I am a project manager for CitiSearch Media. I have a dog that I jog with at least three times a week and let's see...

Chris: You forgot to mention beautiful and that's the truth.

Mai: So you like my dog I see. Well what do you think of me?

75

Chris: Keno is cool, the truth of the matter is the comment was directed at you but you already knew that.

Mai: Yeah but it is nice to hear. Now it's your turn.

Chris: Hmm. Okay I got it. I'm 22, about 5'9 maybe 5'10. I'm a college graduate...

Mai: Fa real.

Chris: (*with a smile*) ...don't interrupt. I'm a writer, I like to sing. I don't smoke either. Chiantis are good but I prefer a nice Riesling. I have no birth children. I am the Youth Events Director for the Boys and Girls Club. Even though I don't have any children of my own, they seem to be naturally drawn to me. In the market anywhere I don't care where it is, kids just look at me and see the word toy across my forehead. Oh my minute is up right?

Mai: That's okay I'm taking in all that I've heard. I am really glad I came now.

So wrapped up in the present company Chris has forgotten about his friends upstairs. Airicka gets a visit from Brevin whose presence releases that uncomfortable 3rd wheel feeling. Although, it is a well-balanced atmosphere, Mysary still shows concern for Airicka until she gives the okay.

Derik: Hey bae you want to dance?

Miz: Sure. (*Whispering in Airicka's ear*) if you're not here when I get back be good.

Airicka: You know me.

Miz: That's why I said it (*As she is being pulled onto the dance floor*)

Brevin: Another one of those secret conversations?

Airicka: Secret? No secrets here, just girl talk that's all.

Brevin: I see. So let me say congrats shorty.

Airicka: What you going to say? You proud of me?

Brevin: Whatever clown. Let me guess, your plans are to catch up on some sleep right?

Airicka: And you know this.

[Airicka] How can I resist? Even him just sitting there is sexy as hell. Can he see it in my face where I want this night to end? It can't go down like that again. Why not? I mean he knows where we stand. No feelings, just friends. Who am I kidding? I luv him. He is the one person that has been both the life and death of my belief in freedom. How can you stop what you want when it's both unbelievably wrong but so damn right? The harder I try to deny this, the deeper I seem to fall into us again. The physical way matures me undoubtedly and affirms what I thought I wanted. He knows my hurts and helps me to leave these tears behind but this burning inside to be done with that old life is not a passing fad or some experimentation. I know who I am but Shit he... (*interrupting her train of thought*)

Brevin: I thought you were going to get a degree in sleep, the way you were always telling me how late you were for this and that. I mean why set your clock an hour ahead if you still ain't going to be late.

Airicka: Whatever. So I was surprised to hear from you.

Brevin: Why, did you think I was mad or something?

Airicka: Nah, were you? Last I heard you went to Kansas doing a show or something.

Brevin: You did invite me to graduation. Did you think I would miss it. I mean when I was going for my nail tech certification and all, you were the only one who I could count on to get through. The least I could do is show luv for my girl.

[Airicka] Brevin and I, I guess you could say we are like some psychotic twisted mind fuck, both wanting not to need each other the way we do. We never committed to a real relationship, it's just been a given ours is a special kind of situation. What am I saying? This is not a flaming disaster screaming head first into a collision course with butterflies. This goes on and has gone on for some time. But you understand don't you? We are we and that is us in its simplest form. No questions asked.

78

Airicka: So that was you yelling out at graduation like some fool.

Brevin: Fa sho. What! I mean, I know they say save your applause for the end but then how you going to know who's cheering for you. Besides what are they going to do anyway, expel me? I am a grown ass man.

Airicka: You so dumb. So how was the trip?

Brevin: It was long but beneficial

Airicka: Beneficial? Right!

Brevin: What does that mean? Forget it, I don't want to know.

Airicka: Niggah, I know your meaning of beneficial.

Brevin: Whatever. How long you planning to stay?

Airicka: The night is still young and I've only had my first drink.

Brevin: Man I'm talking about now that you graduated, you lush. *Just then the DJ interrupts the regularly scheduled jam with a[8] Soca rhythm everybody knows and as if possessed Airicka as do many others who are seated storm the dance floor. Skirts hiked to the edge of thighs waists bend slowly, hips twist and move as the music hypnotizes the people to obey without reservation. The slow start allows the amateurs*

---

[8] Play track "Dolla Wine" as you read

79

to be caressed carefully into comprehension. The words awaken the body with sounds the soul is aching to hear. Resistance is futile. The tempo, a unique blend of heart pounding drums and light-hearted bells like "French Kiss" in reverse moving is almost involuntary. You pray that this moment won't end. The words out of the speakers are like gospel and as if it were the melodies of that pipe organ you hear "She sezin' don like the pace. We movin' too slow. She wanta work out the waist. Raise the tempo..." Brevin spins Airicka around and pulls her with the intent to want her. She is not easily controlled, the music is her lover anyone else is a burden. Airicka hikes up her skirt to give her the space to pop her hips and waist. It is controlled pandemonium erupting on the floor, now a sea of bodies intertwined with the music move back forth, left and right. This goes on for what feels like 30 minutes and as the song finally fades, an easily mingled massage of saxophone breathes across the floor.

Brevin enjoyed the grind but he will not be denied this moment. With the swell of the saxophone, he places his hand on her waist drawing her in to him. He looks into her with a passion in his eyes that suggest feelings never really spoken before. It was like the whole world stopped to pay homage to one breath. The strength of her will smashes against the calm in his assurance. As the snare and keys drip against the shifting color of the squared circle. Before any words are spoken their hands arrange whisper and form color that can only be uttered as beautifully sexy. Between the darkness you could hear the power pulling from this type of comfort. Then the beat and the words began to swirl around. Everyone else seems to disappear. On the dancefloor it's the music, the passion, and the two of them. The conflict of want and denial is clearly crushed into oblivion.

80

[Airicka]Okay, this is too much. Come on girl pull away, but I miss this so much. Remember the morning after the last time you needed this? It's like all of him grabs me with the weight of 7 million tiny volcanos. His heart beat fills the gaps in my pulse. Airicka you know how this is going to end up, we can not go out like this again. We finally got everything going right. You not even listening to yourself any more are you? Like the smell of that perfect night breeze captured in a touch, he believes me back into his fantasy with a slow wine then endearing drag of his hand to support me. Crooning in my ear...

Brevin: ...[9]♪♫You can go any place you want. To fancy clubs and restaurants. But I can only watch you with her. My nose pressed up against the window-pane ♪♫.

It is more the thought behind his efforts than it is his singing. Creating an atmosphere where the aroma of friendship vanishes in an instant. The strength behind his embrace captures security, serenity, and the comforting storm of unbridled passion as the slow melodic tenor marinades and begins to soak into her skin. Escape is not an option as basic thought is even a task that can not be achieved.

Brevin: ♪♫I want to be the one that you just can't live without. I want to be the one that you never fit on out. I want to be the one that you let give you the loving♪♫

There was a time when Airicka and Brevin were the perfect imperfect couple. When they weren't fighting they were fucking. It didn't start

---

[9] Listen to the song "I Who Have Nothing" L. Vandross

*that way though. They met at a house party. Airicka turned all the guys
down who asked her to dance. Before she could turn Brevin down he
offered to make her 2 drinks, if she didn't think one was
awesometacular he would go outside and moon the next car that
passed by. One [10]Shake that Ass,Cherry Fucker Shot, and a sitation for
indecent exposure, and a later confession the drink was great they
ended up a in a Double T laughing about it. To this day she never lets
him live it down especially when they spot a police car. Airicka didn't
want to be tied down but she hated when Brevin talked about his other
female friends. Brevin treated Airicka like she was the only one in the
world that mattered. It wasn't with gifts and things. He was bad
enough to tell her sit your ass down, which he often said when she tried
to lean, grinch or scream on him. You could say Brevin was the only
real constant man in her life. You could say they were each other's fall
back when the moment called for it. Despite the insanity without say
they deep down cared for one another. She will never say, but when
their relationship broke up she was really heart broken. Keeping him
around is a way to sooth the pain.*

*Airicka unable to create words, her eyes are allowed to fall silent as
she tries to pull away. He reaffirms his commitment by relaxing the
pressure but adding more comfort to the embrace. Unable to take it
she tears away and walks quickly through the crowd and to the Ladies
Room. The music is so strong it begins to permeate through the walls.
As if his arms never left, Airicka continues to drown in the memory.
Alone for the moment she leans on the counter, looking into the mirror
then she begins to release the pain in one single tear drop...*

---

[10] Recipes: Shake that Ass (p.297) Cherry Fucker (p.297)

Back at the table Mysary and Derik see no signs of Christopher, Airicka or Brevin.

Derik: Hey babe, since everybody seems to have left already I was wondering if I could take you somewhere so we can talk.

Miz: Where did you have in mind?

Derik: Just come with me.

Miz: Well whose car are we taking?

Derik: I'll drive and we'll take yours okay. Just let me get something out of my car right quick. And so you're not worried, I'll have Donte' drop my car off at the house so we don't have to comeback to this side of town.

Miz: Oh so you've thought of everything umph? Don't think you got a handle on me, remember the rules.

Derik: (*with a hint of sarcasm*) Yes, if a man for any reason thinks he knows the rules, it is a woman's porogative to add or change the rules at any time without prior notification.

Miz: I see you've been studying. So where are we going again?

Derik: I didn't tell you? Oh my bad.

Miz: Cute real cute. Don't make me call my other friend.

Derik: He told me about this place. Hey, so why don't you lay back and relax. I got this.

[Mysary] The one thing that makes Derik so damn sexy is his take-charge type of attitude. When I feel flighty about the simplest of things his thought is let's make it happen. Of course that's all thanks to me.

Running her fingers up the back of her neck locking them into pillow form, Derik chooses this moment to lay the first steps in a carefully devised plan. Selecting the "To the Point Jamz" playlist on the iPod, the silver toned darkness and the Kenwood speakers amplify the melody of the perfect kick off Jam "Lady in my Life". Instantly putting a smile on her face, Derik never looks he just anticipates her reactions from songs to come. The drive normally takes 20 minutes but to keep the spirit of the moment, he takes the more round about approach. As the night breeze rushes slow it creates a new background that brings even more life to the already awesome soundtrack. There are no real words said at the moment the nonverbal communications do all the relating. Each song running together overlapping like one long piece eliciting continuous smiles and thoughts of where will this night end as they continue and drive off into the darkness...

It's later that night, some are still partying hard but the bulk of the people have paired up and have gone their way and some have let the party spill over into the the local iHop, Denny's, or HoJos. Mai offers Chris a ride home to continue the conversation and because both his roommates were clearly nowhere to be found. After saying a few goodbyes to classmates and associates, they leave. No one who is really in the inner circle has had the opportunity to see this new woman attached to Chris. Just like two old friends the conversation in the car is still fervent and strong. You would never believe that they met just a few days ago. The undertone of the quiet storm seems to blare with a clarity that is almost ironic or like a prelude to what is happening to the two of them. "Conversations to theme music", I am sure this has never happened to you, so you will have to take my word for it, when I say this is on some other level.

Finally reaching the door of course, they sit in the car for about an hour still talking and laughing. They have probably said goodbye about 6 of 7 times now, only to welcome a whole new conversation. What started in the car with the motor running is now some hour and 30 minutes later before the motor gets turned off. Instead of goodbye, the conversation continues to the front porch. The soft smell of a clear spring night frees the air to create an awakening of comfort. The house sits on a small piece of land separated on all sides maybe about 10 yards away from the main streets. Most of the homes are owned by families and have been around for generations. So other than a few seniors and some young business professionals most of the neighborhood is quite calm. Chris invited Mai to sit on the hanging chair where they have a view of the night and are shaded from the direction of the breeze.

Mai: Wow, the sky is really clear tonight.

Chris: Yeah, I've spent many a nights out here just trying to clear my head.

Getting the sense Mai maybe a little chilly Chris responds by grabbing the hand knitted camel hair throw from the basket next to the door. Placing it around Mai hoping to draw her closer to him. Appreciating the sentiment when she offers to share, he undoubtedly accepts the invitation. She then turns and nestle her back into his chest creating a moment of exhausted bliss. Before relaxing into that final position of comfort she inquires if this is okay. Bound by the utter joy of comfort, trapped beneath the silence of manifested dreams, Chris plays it cool and returns it's all good.

Mai: This is real nice. Something about this feels good.

Chris: Fa sho'.

Mai: So I noticed tonight at Sheila's that you have a lot of female friends. Is there anything I need to know before we go further.

Christopher: Nah, it's all good.

Mai: Ok, you sure there ain't no poems I'm going to hear saying, "I used to love her". (*With a hint of laughter*)

Christopher: So what you saying? (*Partially serious not really sure if the joke is a joke or not.*)

Mai: A little offensive are we?

Christopher: Never that. On the real I get questioned about that from time to time. I must admit it does bother me to some degree. I know most men with a lot of female friends are usually gaming on them or gay. As far as men go, I got two that I run with and that I know in any situation, they got my back. Other than, that dudes ain't my cup of tea.

Mai: Any reason?

Christopher: Honestly, I know this is said often but for me it seems to be true. I am not like other guys in that I like the things outside the norm. You know, ballroom dancing and the appreciation of a good wine over strip clubs and Courvoisier. Some guys do things to get girls. I just do me. Yeah I can sing and I'm artistic but there is more to this than using my skills to game on skins or something. Dudes always asking how many women you got? Or they get upset thinking I'm gaming on their girls or something.

Mai: Is it just the girl factor that you don't get along or is there more?

Chris: Well there is more. Why do you ask?

Mai: I didn't know if it was that alpha male thing.

Chris: Relationships and religion are the top two reasons I sometimes have issues. I mean I get a long with dudes, we just don't make that friend thing a big deal like women do.

Mai: And what is that supposed to mean?

Chris: You know what I mean.

Mai: If I did I would not have asked.

Chris: Sure, okay I believe that. This is no down to women in any way. They tend to have more girlfriends and most of the guys I know keep it to about 2 to 4 tops. When I see women out they travel in numbers. Enough about me, lets get back to what we were talking about in the car. You mean to tell me, you have never tried black linguini?

Mai: Oh you going to just flip the topic like that and I am supposed to just go along with it?

Chris: Yes.

Mai: If I said no, then what?

Chris: Then you say no. It ain't that deep.

Mai: You giving in pretty easy sir.

Chris: Oh I think you misunderstood. We are still moving in the direction I chose. It is just noted that you objected.

Mai: Hm. Anywho! So are you going to cook this black linguini for me?

Chris: Sure. Are you allergic to seafood or anything I should know about?

Mai: None that I know of. Let the record show I can eat.

Chris: You continue to amaze me.

Mai: What? ThatI like to eat?

Chris: Nah,that you would just put it out there like that. On the real, it's cool.

Mai: Don't let the size fool you.

Chris: Okay then.

Mai: Anything else you want to know?

Chris: Whatever you are willing to share.

The freshness of this day simmered to a nice cool that smelled of peace. Sitting looking out on the early morning skyline something strange happens. Unlike any other woman before she just opens up like that first bloom in spring. Not in a way that is confessional or crazy. This is very natural and comfortable. Chris' presence has this quality of making you feel restful and then the words just flow out.

Mai: There is not much to say. I mean I'm a simple girl. It's been a few years since I've been in a relationship.

Christopher: Any reason?

Mai: Cute. My last relationship took a lot out of me. I gave too much of myself to the point it became hard to breathe. You know how it is when you hook up with that person and all you want is to be together and the more people try to cause confusion the tighter you become.

Christopher: Yeah.

Mai: His mom considered me family, treated me like a daughter. We had been through so much together that when it ended I... I went into this deep depression. To tell the truth I never felt this comfortable around anyone before to talk about this. I know you don't really want to hear about some other guy so I'll stop...

Christopher: I don't want to talk about it if it will upset you. But I'm cool if you are. I do enjoy listening to your voice though. It seems as if this talk is helping you out.

Mai: Well, I do enjoy your company. No pun intended. So what do we talk about now?

Christopher: Let me ask a question, what would a guy like myself have to do to get a woman such as you?

Mai: Are you applying for the position?

Christopher: I need to set up an official interview right?

Mai: When and where?

Christopher: Tio Pepe's next Thursday night.

Mai: My, my spoil a girl like this and I may look for this treatment all the time, you sure you can hang?

Christopher: What you mean?

Mai: I mean a romantic night of good conversation, dinner at a fancy Italian restuarant, and promises of black linguini dinners, a girl could come to expect this treatment on the regular. You sure you want to use all your tricks on our 1st date.

Christopher: Well technically that will be our 2nd and 3rd dates. And to the other thing trix are for kids. This here is grown folks biz. Just wait and see.

Mai: Oh I see. Impressive. Most impressive.

Christopher: Yes, Lord Vader.

Mai: Ok you have just banked some serious cool points for that.

Christopher: Really why?

Mai: You are the first guy, to catch that. Yes I am a Star Wars GEEK!

Christopher: Episodes 4 -6 right?

Mai: You know!

Christopher: Wow, so I got a few more keys to the puzzle. Hmmm?

Mai: What does that mean?

Christopher: Nothing. I see that you are one of them cute geeks.

Mai takes this time to shift the subject a little in an attempt to find out more information about the type of guy Christopher really is. What better way than to set a scenario. Carefully laid questions with a guided motive, rather than just ask direct questions.

Mai: Chris, can I share something with you?

Chris: Sure.

Mai: What if I told you I had a child.

Chris: I thought I met him in the park this morning.

Mai: I'm serious.

Chris: And?

Mai: You wouldn't have anything to say?

Loaded questions like these often test to see what kind of person you are. With her current position, she could detect any change in breathing patterns or sudden pauses in a response. The seed of insecurity can be laid at anyone's door.

The real challenge is will it take root.

Chris: Look I understand things happen. I really like you and even though we just started talking I hope we get a chance to see where things lead.

Responding to her before making it verbal she is unable to sense if there is a hidden message in what is said. Awaiting a response the breath between each millisecond stretched to the point of pause. This always creates an uneasy feeling within Chris.

Mai: Well, I do have a child but not like you think.

Chris: What do you mean?

Mai: My mother had me when she was 16. And although she enjoyed motherhood she enjoyed partying a little bit more. I was about 3 or 4 when she started putting me with my grandmother or anyone of her friends that wasn't able to go the club that night. As I got older I pretty much had to fend for myself. Sometimes I felt as if I was a burden to her you know? She never said it but if I wasn't there I don't think it would've bother her one bit. She provided food and clothes and stuff but my grandmother was the one who told me about the birds, the bees and all the little princess treasure things. When I turned 12, she got pregnant again with my little sister. I would find out my purpose in life at this point. It was to provide free childcare so my mother could party and go out drinking.

Chris: Well what about your dad?

Mai: Not much to say really. I have seen him twice in my entire life. Once when I was three and the second time was when I was 16. The interesting thing is I can remember exactly down to the letter what he was doing when I was 3 and I was about 50 yards away. But I don't remember what he looked like when I was sitting across from him less than 2 feet at age 16. My sister's father was there for about 2 maybe 3 years before he was Audi. You want to know what the most painful part of the whole thing was?

Chris: Are you okay to talk about it?

Mai: What do you mean?

Chris: If you want to talk about it, cool. I just don't want to bring up something that may hurt you or bring you down. Know what I'm saying?

Mai: It's all good. [So I thought] As I was saying, what was I saying again?

Oblivious to the fact that she is trying to see if he really has been listening, Chris being the person he is, recounts everything almost verbatim to the point where she was about to unveil something seriously painful.

Chris: …You were saying the most painful part was…

Mai: Oh, my mother made me feel like it was my fault that men didn't want to stay. I couldn't understand. She caught one of her so-called

94

best friends messing around with one her dudes and a few months later they were going out to the club together. Without even asking I was left to watch my little sister and that same friend's 3 bad ass kids. I was treated like the bad guy in the picture no matter what I did it was never good enough...

Like the fragile petals of rare flower, slowly as the words fall from her lips, she begins to breakdown. Who would have ever thought that on the first night she would be comfortable enough to be so candid?

Mai: She always told me she couldn't wait till I was pregnant so I could see what a no good child like myself was like. The whole time I was in high school she accused me of having sex while she was at work and that any day she was going to get the word that I was pregnant. It got to the point where even her conversations with her friends would always end up with them almost guessing when I would get pregnant. She never realized how much that hurt me...

As if he already knew how, Chris lends his body and shoulder to brace her. His hands suggest strength with his arms creating the caress of security. It is moments like this that our frailties open us up to the core.

Mai: I'm sorry. I didn't mean to spoil such a wonderful night. Please forgive me.

Chris: It's cool. I'm amazed you feel comfortable enough to share that with me. You know?

Mai: I don't know what it is about you. Something just feels so real. If that make sense?

Chris: It does.

Mai: What time is it?

Chris: Um, a little after 3. Wow it doesn't seem like we've been talking that long.

Mai: I know. Guess when the company's good time flies.

Chris: I know you have to go…

Mai: It's a wonder you have any energy left. What you on speed or something. Don't crash too hard, I would like to see you again this week.

Chris: Definitely. Hey, next Saturday you should come by and check out my singing group at Sheila's.

Mai: One of my coworkers was telling me about Sheila's and how she heard this really hot group there called Unified, United something like that. Anyway what's the name of your group?

Chris: UNiTY!

Mai: Ooops, my bad. I didn't offend you did I?

Chris: Nah, in fact if you would've heard some of the names people called us, you would trip. It's all good, at least word is getting out.

Mai: Yeah I'll swing by for a bit before I have to go off to work. Well as much as I am enjoying this, I should be getting home and you have a lot of sleep to catch up on, I guess. Right?

Chris: I wish. I took some time off for graduation and all. I hope I get to see you before next Saturday.

Mai: (*With a slow "Well"*) That would depend on you and how bad you want really want to see me. So what happened to our interview at Tio Pepe's next Thursday, or were you just playing?

Chris: Oh we are definitely on for Thursday! What? Say about 6:30 - 7:00?

Mai: Make sure you bring references.

Walking Mai to her car slowly, they enjoy every minute continuing the small talk and amazed by the fact that they've spent hours talking and still have more to say. Though they both want to kiss they simply share a really nice embrace to say goodbye again. Watching as her car turns the corner, smiling Chris walks back to the porch. Just as he was cleaning up and was preparing to go in the house, Mysary pulls up. Taking a few minutes to gather her things, she notices Chris as he is going in the house. Figuring it was no more than one of his normal late night writing moments she thought nothing of it as she followed suit. Their paths cross again for the first time since the graduation party at Shelia's literally the day before.

Chris: Hey.

Miz: What [yawn] up? Whoah, this was a long day.

Chris: Yo [laughing] it's already tomorrow.

Miz: I know I couldn't do that again. I am worn out and you know I'm too tired to take a bath. As sleepy as I am right now, I just might drown. Anybody call?

Chris: I don't know. I haven't check the messages yet.

Miz: Well they can wait til later.

The rush of such a wonderful night is for the moment suppressed under the nagging desire to find out if he is the last card caring member of the V Club. Their friendship was never predicated on the fact that they would share intimate information. It was just one of the unwritten rules in this relationship. They both agreed to wait until they were married but they also said if for any reason one of them broke the promise they would tell the other. On the flip side, he has wanted to tell Miz about Mai all day and for some reason with the thoughts in his head it doesn't seem like the right time. Torn between two ideas neither coming to the forefront of his side of the conversation before he adjourns to his room Mysary is reminded of a thought.

Miz: Hey you wanted to talk to me about something earlier today you remember what it was.

Chris: It can wait.

Miz: Sure? (*Yawn*)

Chris: Yeah man, see you in the morning.

Miz: I don't have to go to work until 5. Dude I aint waking up til 3 maybe 4.

Chris: You stupid. So you I guess your going to Holy Homes Missionary Cathedral?

Miz: More like Bedside Baptist Holy Rest Communion Church with Pastor Prophet Reverend Goose Down.

Chris: Night man.

Miz: Holla.

They both head into their own rooms, this time neither tired but both amazed by their nights. Interesting both chose not to share the events of the night with the other. Chris lying in his bed, Miz in hers, both looking at the ceiling they smile. Then Chris' phone vibrates. Checking the message, desperately wanting it to be Mai. It's Mysary saying, thank you again for the gift. Just as he is about to respond, a new message comes through. This time it's Mai sending a picture and a message "Thanx for a great night. Here's a little something to remember me by. Sweet dreams" and that is how the night ends.

Why is it that the first full week after you graduate is the craziest? You got to deprogram yourself from thinking you got something to do or somewhere to be at such and such a time. Doing nothing is so foreign that you conjure up a task to do. Most of your friends are working at times when you're not and vice versa or like you they are graduates and they have no plans but to sleep, eat and maybe look for a job. If you have things planned for the day, the time between tasks seems so long it's maddening. Chris wakes up early everyday while Miz's regiment requires the typical alarm snooze smash and throw exercise followed by the last minute rush and recover. Airicka holds down three part-time jobs so rarely is she seen before noon on most days and 3 on others. While they were in school and working no matter what, they always found time to hook up and renew the properties of their friendship. Not so much now, with Miz spending more time with Raven helping with wedding plans, Chris and the band rehearsing at Sheila's preparing for Saturday, and Airicka working like a Hebrew slave.

Everything has been reduced to sending the occasional one-liner text which; usually garners a witty retort from one of the other three. Few even understand the friendly banter between the modern day, Three's Company, nor do they even try. Is it jealousy that making friends for them has not been as fruitful? To ask Chris, Miz and Airicka, how to describe their friendship? Simply the perfect marriage with no sex. We now join two friends already in progress, crossing paths. Chris is on his way out the door not before saying later to Airicka and a what up to Brevin, who are reclined in the living room. You can tell they've

100

been talking for a minute or so. Her body lain in defiance of
conversation, he sitting somewhat lifeless on the floor. Once the door
closes it seems as if it's an all clear and they return the land of 1,000
conversations that seem to go nowhere fast. As if trying to come to
some resolve Airicka ask...

Airicka: Brevin what do you want from me? If you think this is the
part where I cry, you picked up the wrong story.
Frustrated by the subtle cander he looks at her with a bit of what are
you saying?

Brevin: You should know me better than that.

In actuality she does. The macho nature carries him but so far because
he truly is a man. Like all good men there are some faults and or flaws.

Airicka: So, I'm asking you what you, Brevin Devon Simmons the
Third wants me to do?

Pit-tiling in that lost child look, he hunches his shoulders slightly as he
continues to sit on the floor. We never say exactly what we want. Why
is that? Anyway, just then the front door opens and Mysary enters in
her usual manner. Before heading up the stairs she can see Airicka and
Brevin both on the floor sitting and talking. Only spotting Airicka ...

Miz: Reeka', wait till I tell you....Oh, hey Brevin.
Looking at me with a quickness she knew all she need to know, which
was girl I'll tell you later. The amazing things is I had to move away
from a home where the women of my family, aunts, and cousins

included ruled to really find a sister who could feel what I'm saying with just a look and vice versa. With the sign everything is cool I got this, Miz resigns to her room.

Airicka: Look Brevin I got to go. There is nothing for me here.

[Airicka In thought]Before I could realize what I was saying I had already thrown the dagger through his heart.

Brevin: Yo Airicka, that's what you think of me, nothing. Nah Nah i'm sayin though what about all the junk I put up with. You crying in my arms over that chic when you said you were over her. Yo and what-about, when I went all the way to your grandparents house and pretended like I was gay. Knowing I was taking the heat off you. All that meant nothin' to you. I ain't goin' out like no punk or nutin' but on the real I gave up a lot for you shorty

Airicka:...And I appreciate all that you've done.

[Airicka In thought]I know this isn't the most opportune time but I wonder if he'll give me one for the road.

Airicka: You've really been one of my best male friends. But, this right here ain't about you though. It's a me thing. You know how bad I want it anyway.

Brevin: Fa' real! I'm trippin' this is for the birds.

Airicka: Hold up now you know I ain't the type to go runnin' after nobody...

Brevin: Yo why you always assume the worst. Like somebody's tryin' to leave you. I was talkin' bout my tude man. You know you my heart and this hurts more than you could ever know.

[Airicka In thought] He thought he could change me. Well at least I think that was his motive. I could always count on him to be on the up and up even when some of the choices I made truly upset him. He never tried to run game or play high post . Brevin didn't have to beg for it or anything the girls wanted him and he knew it. Using that to his advantage i'm sure there weren't that many lonely nights.

Airicka: So why don't you talk to me for a change.

Brevin: This ain't one of those after school specials niggah and you ain't high profile yet.

Airicka: You was the one lookin' like somebody pissed in your wheaties.

Brevin: You this always happens when we get to talking about you, me, and any possible plans.

The air in the room is finally lightened to the point of smiles exchanged. Sitting down next to Brevin Airicka places her hands on his to candidly persuade comfort and affection.

Brevin: So when you you leavin'?

Airicka: Why?

Brevin: You planning to see your Pops before you bounce?

Airicka: I thought about it.

The punctuation of this statement could not be captured on paper.
Let's just say that the subject was closed with a quickness.

Brevin: Forget I ask, so when you leaving again?

Airicka: Two weeks, you gonna help me move?

Brevin: You know I will if you need.

[Airicka In thought] Where would I be with out him. Oh yeah, I would still think that it's only supposed to last 15 minutes. Why do I have penis on the brain? It has been awhile hasn't it?

Airicka: For real? I wasn't serious. What…you gonna drive up to Queens with me? Then what you gonna do drive back by yourself?

Brevin: Nah, one of my peeps lives in Corona. i'll stay a few days with her then maybe drive back.

[Airicka]What.. the... This niggah gonna tell me bout some trick up State he gonna stay with? Knowing him it's a steady piece for him. It's like he just makes female friends for the fun of it.

Airicka: So how long have you known her?

Brevin: Who?

Airicka: The Avon lady! The girl in Corona who else?

Brevin: Oh Paige, bout 6 -7 years. She used to teach here. We met at the spot on Charles Street and we kinda hit it off from there. Know what I mean?

[**Airicka**] Hell yeah I know what you mean. You were hittin' her switches like you were fixed with Hydraulics. Why the hell did I ask? I must be a gluten for mental punishment. I don't want to know about some other chic you doin'.

Brevin: After you get situated maybe we can go to the Village for some Falafel?

Airicka: Sure. Or we could hit up that juice bar on 127th you feel me?

Brevin: Oh hell yeah. You know what I could really go for, a veggie pattie...

Airicka & Brevin: and some coco bread!

Airicka: You owe me ...

Brevin: ...Hot sex on a platter. Right?

Airicka: You would like that wouldn't you?

Brevin: Hi I'm Brevin this must be your first time meeting me.

105

Airicka: Shut up!

[**Airicka**] Oh don't think you're slick changing the subject. How can he pass it off like he didn't say nothing, Humph. Wait a minute now who's trippin'?

With a life riddled with cliché's there seems to be moments where levity is the estranged mistress that brings some sort of balance or peace. Even the thought of another woman in the mind of a casual friend can create a depreciation of value. There is something about wanting to be the only one that feeds a growing desire of acceptance.

Brevin: You know I haven't given you a pedicure in a long time.

Airicka: Yeah now that's what i'm talking about. "Did you bring your stuff?"

[**Airicka**] Damn, Miz and I finished off the last bottle of wine the other day.

Brevin: It's in my trunk. Oh man you won't believe it I just got this new bottle of Bettinelli from this winery a few miles south of here.

Airicka: Meet me upstairs in my room.

[**Airicka**] A straight man who can professionally give a pedicure is really off the chain and dangerous. Girls beware of those Brevin type men. Good guys are the most dangerous of all. On the surface they are calm real low key. Some of you may even mistake them for punks or assume they are no threat. This is where the good guys perfect their strategy. Any guy can be there when your man isn't and say all they common lines to ease the tension. But a real good guy can entice you with a sort of candid indirectness that really blows your mind.

Brevin cooks exotic dishes and knows in detail what wines compliment them. For example he made this [11]Fusilli Pomodoro, you would have sworn it came out of one of those fancy resturants with the designer linen. He is a licensed nail tech and masseuse. He has exquisite taste in flowers and to top it off he's only 28 and he has no children. So you ask why are men like this not taken? Because their's is an endless search for a woman that is truly mission improbable...the one who is secure in herself in ALL facets of her being. No one woman satisfies this insatiable romantic; so alas they find solace in the confines of many. So he's that guy at work who sends a lady fugimums and gerber daisies for no reason and always brings his lunch in clean Tupperware, that when heated in the microwave wraps orgasmic circles around your taste buds and it's not leftovers from Applebee's. You be careful he may be one of them.

As for me I know I shouldn't, but the things that man can make my body do? All I can say is um! Um! UMM! He's asked me to move in with him with no strings. I know there is more to it than what he is saying. I'm not Susie Homemaker by a long shot and I don't think his laundry list of women would eventually bother me. Anywho he's back...

---

[11] Recipe: Fusili Pomodoro (p.290)

Brevin: Are you ready?

On the other side of town it's a break from the rehearsal now is the time for Chris to call Mai who is working now but should be about ready to break for lunch. Waiting to be connected to her department Chris still gets a measure of butterflies because of the newness of this relationship.

Mai: This is Maya

Christopher: (*Moderately disguising his voice*) Yes ma'am I was interested in acquiring a sit down luncheon with you so we can discuss the futures of Company Luv Industries.

(*With a smile on her end and light laughter on his the two find a mutual joy in the sound of the others voice*)

Christopher: Can you talk now or do I need to call you back?

Mai: Everything is cool.

Chris: I just wanted to see if you were busy for lunch today.

Mai: Yeah, the boss is taking everybody out to celebrate one of the section leaders birthdays. I would try to get out of it but I am the boss. Why? What's up?

Chris: Nothing.

Mai: So you called me to see if I was busy for lunch for no other reason than personal inquiry? Right! *With a bit of sarcasm*

Chris: Nah man, we were breaking for lunch and I knew you went to lunch about now so…

Mai: You thinking about little ol' me? I'm flattered Mr. Company.

Chris: You know, I was hoping not to loose any cool points for calling so soon.

Mai: Well I'm glad you were willing to sacrifice for me. So did you write anymore of those sexual pancake poems?

Chris: Well, when I see you tomorrow night you'll find out.

Now everyone in the office is ready to leave and again in the midst of a good conversation it must end too soon. They agree to talk later and bid adu with unseen matching smiles. Chris grabs a bite from the falafel stand down the street from Sheila's. The rest of the Band orders from Crazy John's sending Sam on the food run. A text from Mai to Chris' phone triggers a smile. Tischa tries to be nosy and get to the bottom of it but that is when the food arrives so it will keep.

Across town Miz and Raven stop at the Juice Bar for the weekly shot of Peach Mango Smoothies and wedding plan meetings.

Raven: What did you think of the place? I know you must thinking that it is alotta money and all and we said we are trying to spend wisely but when I saw the waterfall and the gazebo, I knew it was it. I can see the pictures now of just coming down the aisle.

Mysary: The place was beautiful. Did you know that if you have your wedding on a Sunday, the price is almost cut in half?

Raven: Stop lying. How did you find that out?

Mysary: I talked to the coordinator while you were off looking at the reception area with the caterer. I told her that you and Wendall were planning to go to law school and you all had to pay everything out of pockets. She said to me, that as a special most, host places offer their space for a discount on Sundays. She was also telling me that everybody wants that Friday-Saturday date so much that they never have a problem booking, even when someone cancels. Sundays are that much harder to fill with everybody going to church and all so they can afford to cut the cost to attract business.

Raven: You know you my girl right? I still wasn't sure how I was going to tell Wendall the cost. You just made this that much easier, what would I do without you.

Mysary: You just make sure you look out for me when it's my turn.

Raven: So what has Derik said about you staying or leaving?

Mysary: We haven't really said anything to each other about the future. I'm still contemplating those two job offers. I mean if I go to Virginia, I'll be close to my sister and that will cut down on living costs.

Raven: Yeah, but you know how much of a free spirit you are. How long will that last?

Mysary: What's that supposed to mean? Oh, you don't think I could stay with my folks for a minute?

Raven: You were the one who always claim to be the dark horse of the family and you know we both only been able to handle the family thing in small doses. I mean, of course they will let you stay but how long could you deal with not having your own space to do whatever you feel like whenever you feel like? Answer that?

Mysary: You right. I don't know who I was fooling. I love my people but I couldn't stay with them for more than a minute. If me and my mommy could run off somewhere and my father would visit on occasion for a few minutes, that would be nice.

Raven: Too true. Ida would totally be down with them conjugal visits. You know?

Mysary: Oh Eva had your youngest sister when? Thank you. She's my hero! Still pushing kids out at 42 and still looking good at 52! I want to be like her when I grow up.

Raven: Momma don't play around!

Mysary: That's going to be you and Wendall don't worry.

Raven: I don't know sometimes.

Mysary: What is it this time?

Raven: What makes you think something is up?

Mysary: I don't know, the fact is that I know you better than you know you sometimes. Come on what's going on?

Raven: I don't know, I think he tried to get a lower grade on the LSAT on purpose.

Mysary: What? You got to be kidding? Why?

Raven: You know we both got accepted to Columbia and Stanford. Well when we found out we would have to pay for grad school ourselves, that's around the time he proposed. He said if we have to do this together we should be together full time and legally.

Mysary: Okay, I don't see what that has to do with the LSAT.

Raven: Well, you know how security is my thing?

Mysary: Yeah me too.

Raven: So when we discussed how we were going to make this work he suggested that one of us would go to community college and take some courses and work while the other goes to school full time. When things level out as far as finances the one working would transfer in to school.

Mysary: Rae,…

Raven: Yeah as stubborn as we both are I thought it was more important that he go to school first because He will be the man of the house and I am supposed to support his vision. Not that I am going to play the barefoot pregnant role. But I see him taking care of business then I could pull up the rear.

Mysary: Needless to say he did not see it that way

Raven: At first, I thought it was about the whole pride thing. You know, thinking he was feeling uncomfortable about a woman supporting you financially?

Mysary: Right.

Raven: His argument was (*altering her voice to mimic Wendell*) number 1. How much harder is it for a woman with intelligence and looks to make it in a male dominated field? 2. Once you get things going, if and when we have kids how much harder would it be for you to get back into the work force with all the crazy rules corporate businesses are putting out there? Number 3 and most important; I know how bad you want to work for Smyth, Gaynes & Thomas. (*Returning to her normal voice*) He says let's go after the big fight first and land that one to get me in the door.

Mysary: Yeah, you stuck to your guns. You the only one I know that would have a good man put forth a good argument and good reason to go his way and you still say no. So how long did this go on?

Raven: This went on for a minute. Until he came up with the idea of whoever scored higher on the LSAT would be the person to go to school, no questions asked. There was no way to check if anyone tried to get a low score I know. Just something inside me says he did. When we got our scores back he got a 171 and I got a 172 and all he said was "No questions asked". As if he knew I would suspect something.

Mysary: Rae now you know I got your back in anything, but this right here is borderline Belview.

Raven: I know it sounds crazy and you're the only one I've told, but I feel... I don't know what I feel.

Mysary: Look, the reason why you think that is because Wendall has done so much for you and you feel like this is your chance to pay him back. Trust that he loves you and this is the way God wanted things to go down and neither of you can change that. You know this ain't no Psych eval or nothing but I think you should let it go. If you don't it will eat at you and affect everything you all are working to build.

Raven: You're right, thanks.

Mysary: Whatever, you know how we do.

Raven: For real thanks because I think this is why we were arguing this past week. I got some making up to do.

Mysary: So let me ask you something.

Raven: What? Okay who are you and what did you do with Ms. Independent?

Mysary: Everybody got jokes. I didn't know that the Universoul Circus let the clowns out into the public. You know without their medication.

Raven: Uh duh, what was da question?

Mysary: You stupid, but seriously I've been thinking about Derik and our relationship. You know how long we've been together and how willing he has been to wait. I don't want to anymore. Look I'm not trying to super spiritual or nothing I'm just being honest. I mean, it's not curiosity. I don't feel like I owe him for waiting. I just want to.

It's been about a month and half two months now. This is not that linear time discussed in science class but that relationship time where 3 days of absence is equal to a full month of separation. If you don't see the person as a regular part of your day, you know, at work during lunch, or even on the bus; you begin to think about what they are thinking if they are thinking about you, if they met someone else and how could they not call you. This stuff will make you crazy male or female we may not handle it the same, but we sure as hell think about some of the same things.

Down by the harbor, right before night fall, Chris and Mai are taking a break from the regulars of the weekend to just enjoy time. When two are on the edge of something special, every moment together is a little slice of wonderful. It's all the little things we do in the beginning of a relationship that can make the journey all that you ever wanted or the hardest fall you have ever had. Its not the holding of hands and the buying of gifts, it is when you find yourself so comfortable to just be you and that seconds apart feel like light years. Chris and Mai stop for a Soy Chai on ice then proceed to walk from one end of the pier to the other. The conversation sounds more like vintage friends than the awkward silence of two people still trying to get to know one another. Mai enjoying the moment but unaware of what Chris has planned ...

Mai: Where are you taking me?

Chris: You'll see.

Mai: Oh you're taking me to one of your secret places again?

116

Chris: Secrets are only good if you can share them right?

Mai: So you not going to tell me?

Chris: You will know soon enough.

Mai: You're lucky you cute.

Chris: Whatever! Just bring yourself on.

Mai: Ooo, I love it when you get all caveman and forceful.

This night there was no blanket, no rose petals, no elaborate feets of fancy. It was just the pier and two people in "something", spending a moment communicating.

Chris: You, silly. But seriously we need to talk.

Mai: Okay, what's up?

Chris: I am not really sure how to say this or where to start.

Mai: Take your time. It's really beautiful out here. The lights from the city look so peaceful and the water is relaxing.

Chris: Mai, These past few weeks have really been great. I am so glad we met. [Damn she is fine. Those lips feel like, damn. Damn. DAMN! Is it too soon to tell her about the vow? Would she believe me?]

Mai is not really sure where this is going, the indifference in Christopher's tone makes it hard to detect his direction positive or negative. This could be the moment when the other shoe falls or this could be that moment of commitment, Patience is truly the enemy, but she wants to see where this is going before jumping to any conclusions.

Chris: What if I told you at the end of the summer I will be going over seas for a few months and if I return I want to get my Master's degree.

Mai: So is this a nice way of telling me we are only a summer time thing?

Chris: If it were, would that bother you?

Mai: Well yes, you can't get rid of me just like that.

Chris: I am definitely not trying to get rid of you. I don't know where this… us is going and I would really like to know where you stand in this.

Mai: Are you sure that's what this is all about?

Chris: Trust me, I brought you here to talk about us. I do have an opportunity to go to Africa on a missionary trip and we just started something. The trip isn't for a few months and I've been here in a situation like this before in a way and I want to know that this, sorry us, is worth the time. I would like to know, are you down?

Mai: I will admit. Things between us are moving fast but to be honest I am enjoying the ride. It's like the comfort level is years and it's only been months. Understand I don't give up good things easy and it has been a long time since I've had someone good. I am glad you felt like we are serious enough to consider this is a point we needed to discuss.

Christopher comforted by the sentiment comes up and hugs her from behind. They continue to talk over things. Mai feels his arms and buries her head in his chest. This right here is something special. Luve is no longer lonely she found Company and the two are very cozy.

Quickly its been about 2 months since graduation Chris, Mysary and Airicka still trying to get the grown thing going and life has sadistically twisted things making the everyday a little bit harder than usual. Christopher changes his work schedule to try and fill the space of school but it has put a strain on his transit to practice. Spending time with Mai has been a welcome adjustment with a hint of contradiction. Not seeing Mysary has more than kept his feelings at bay or at least for now, has made them almost non-existent.

Christopher and Mysary have not had the chance to do their usual Sunday brunch where they catch up on the weeks. It has been a minute since they really had the opportunity to talk friend to friend. Graduation seems to have snowballed into life. The brunch on Sunday, they had agreed would be a ritual ever since they got jobs at the Chart House and the Aquarium. Since the 10th grade they have never missed a Sunday. Even when Mysary was on retreat in the Poconos she drove all night just to meet her best friend to find out nothing really happened. See, it was never about the events it was about their commitment to each other they were the best of friends and had been

119

through High school, bad relationships, and crazy parents. Now the rush of life has made it almost impossible for them to bond even for a quick bite. They text from time to time but most phone calls go directly to voicemail or only last long enough to say let me call you right back. Mysary still doesn't know about Maya, Derik is not pressuring her but she can tell he wants to know if she will leave or stay.

*Chris is concerned about what is **this** thing with Mai that is both comforting and scary at the same time. How it's so much more than a feeling and why does it feel as if he is cheating on Mysary? In the past, relationships were a little easier to peg than **this**. For whatever reason, he can't put his finger on it. Mai has done some amazing things in the short time. Finding paying gigs for the band, trusting Chris with picking up her little sister from summer camp, and even helping him get his things in order for the Master's program and the missionary trip which is more than 3 months away. No woman in his past has ever taken a vested interest in Christopher the person. Beyond Mysary, no one ever thought to even ask about anything in his life. Short of dropping the L word or trying to be the first to screw him; Mai's proving to be more than a simple girlfriend she is operating as best friend 2.0.*

Today Christopher and Mai take advantage of the one free moment that intersects their schedules. They are together and time is no factor it's like two old friends hooking up for some fun. There is truly something different about the groundwork being laid here, neither can figure out what it is but they both feel it. Can't you feel it? Maya's sister is spending the week with her father.

120

Rather than go to the movies or anything, they just have a casual conversation in her living room. The deep maroon walls were huddled around hardwood floors centered by two bodies perfectly placed on the olive sectional is the scene. Christopher leaned in a corner, elbow confident on the arm of the sofa positioned so his eyes could make contact with all of her at any time. Maya seated legs crossed bracing a throw pillow between thighs and arms. "Be Sweet On Me" is playing in the background. The Bose series iii keeps the air chilled to a soft rumble.

Chris: So what high school did you go to?

Mai: Western.

Chris: Western Dove? Oh now I see.

Mai: What's that s'pposed to mean?

Chris: Nothing...

Mai: Right? So let me guess (*with a hint of sarcasm*) Mervo, no Lake Clifton, Lithonia High?

Chris: Because you're cute I will let that slide. I rep the castle on the hill to the fullest, ya heard?

Mai: City, A lot of those boys were sweatin' us hard.

Chris: What? How you figure? Doves flock Knights, yall couldn't help

121

it I mean, being next to Poly and all. To tell the truth the City women know how to keep a brother's eye.

Mai: WHATever. So how many doves flocked around you and don't give me that, they were just friends.

Chris: I was having too much fun making my name ring through the halls, to sweat the doves. Besides most of the guys treated the doves like Pringles, just couldn't have just one. I did kind of hook up with this one, but it didn't go anywhere.

Mai: Too stuck up right?

Chris: Not at all, just some people were not meant for a relationship beyond acquaintance. Not really sure if she was feeling me like that.

Mai: You know most guys used to call us heffas, hoes, and pigeons. For a while I almost started to believe them.

Chris: Present company excluded, right?

Mai: Didn't know you then so I can't say. I mean you talk a good game but that was high school and we all did our share of dirt.

Chris: You right on that. So it sounds like you had a lot going on for you. What sport did you play, let me guess track, nah softball right?

Mai: Should have stayed with your first mind. These are the legs of a track star.

Golden calves creep from behind the pillow slowly rising and rotating around left to right beautifully manicured toes. For a moment I was hypnotized by just one leg and as if she knew I was about to return to the land of cohesive thought, the next leg slaps me back into the land of wonderful.

Chris: Very nice. Very, very nice. Humph, so you got any stories about you roaming the school halls?

Mai: Why?

Chris: Hey, I don't want to take you out somewhere and the old captian of the JV team come with static. Then what, the two of you break out into an impromptu race or something or some dude still not over you, wearing your lettermen's jacket...

As he chuckles at himself, I see no need to go there.

Mai: Well you know with all that was going on at home, I never wanted anybody to get too close to me. So, even if the guy was nice it never stood a chance. But Western had its own share of drama. It had to be a man who decided to make it an all girl school.

Chris: Nah, Why you think that? I thought girls get along better than guys. Don't tell me it was all a lie. I mean the very fabric of our existence ...

Mai: Because you're cute...

Chris:… you going to let that one slide right?

Mai: Stop trying to put words in my mouth.

Chris: Words? Never that.

Mai: and what does that mean?

Shunning the obvious insinuation. Although comfortable to a great extent there are still moments where innocence and nerves over rule. As much as he wanted to kiss her, he had a greater fear of where it might lead. Chris quickly changes the topic back to the original focus.

Chris: Why do say a man created all girl schools like that was a problem.

Mai awaiting the advance is a little thrown by the abrupt shift, thinking it's a cute case of nerves. Inside she smiles secretly wanting it as much as he does, she can never let on that she feels this way. Following his lead…

Mai: Despite popular belief, women are catty, vengeful and vindictive. It's not that women get along better than men, we just talk more that's all.

Chris: Are you sure you should be saying this? You know Big Sistah may be watching.

Mai: Never mind.

Chris: What?

Mai: Nothing. (*With a bit of subtle force*)

Chris: Uh oh, the nothing statement.

Mai: What does that mean?

Chris: Just that there is something wrong generally on my part.

Mai: Really? Then what is it?

Chris: Joking a little too much.

Mai: Good recovery.

Chris: Well, you don't live with women most of your life and don't learn something. Hey, let me ask you something, what is one of your not so cool moments?

Mai: You first.

Chris: But I asked the question.

Mai: okay and?

Chris: Oh a'ight then. Here it is… How embarrassing?

Mai: That's totally up to you. You asked the question?

Chris: Cute.

Trying to gage to what extreme is the limit. The delima comes in trying to interpret the last statement. If he tells a dark secret but funny will that establish a new level of trus?. Could he put his foot in his mouth and never recover? What to do in these situations? I mean does anybody really know how to handle this in a split second when you have to make the choice? Pausing for a few, Chris tries to think.

Chris: Okay one night before a performance at my aunt's Church social, we were rehearsing Tomorrow by the Winans. Nah, wait I got one. You know that church up on Pulaski, the white one on the corner?

Mai: Yeah.

Chris: a'ight I was standing there waitin' on the #51. I had my hands in my pocket chillin'. How about the bus was coming and my hands got stuck. That ain't even the half. Yo I pulled so hard I fell off the hill right as the bus pulled up. The driver and everybody laughed. I was on the ground flopping around like a fish.

Chris: You can laugh.

Mai: (*with an inside giggle she tries to regain herself to go on.*) So what happened at the social?

Chris: Wait how I get to give two and you haven't given anything yet? Is this some kind of 2 for 1 special?

126

Mai: Well you started with one then switched it up. Now I want to know. You know you want to tell me, so come on now out with it.

Chris: Sure. You know the song right? Well I started "Jesus Said" and right on time I belched so loud it echoed. We couldn't do the song for a least another month with out laughing hysterically.

Mai: Wow. Seems like you and church don't get along very well.

Chris: Nah, I think G just made me his personal inside joke.

Mai: G? Please explain?

Chris: G and I, we are down like four flats on a dump truck. See when I talk to God it's personal and I got to be me. So I developed my own way of talking to God. I call Him G.

Mai: So twice you got punked by G.

Chris: You say that.

Mai: I did say it and I must admit it is rather funny.

Smiling hard which evolves into contagious chuckles.

[Chris & Maya in thought[12]]

---

[12] Just thought I would reference <u>the Dae the Sun Wouldn't Rise</u>

The rest of this conversation is somewhat of a blur as to who said what.

Somehow we ended up face to face

Maybe it was just fate

How did we end up this way?

What does this mean, do
I make the first move?

What if she thinks it's too soon?

What if he thinks it's too soon

I want this

Does he want this as much as me?

I never thought...

Who could ever imagine

This

She is simply amazing

He is more than I could imagine

Does she like this as much as me?

i mean i really like this

Kiss

128

Both Chris and Mai share the joy and the pleasure locked in that moment as if they knew it was time to go to the next step. Each second was like breathing. A gentle hint of passion enclosed by the erotic whisper of innocence is the only way to explain it. The taste of her lips burns a cold impression that lasts long after the day is gone. The wows of the heart tattoo, the air, and flow between the fingers of existence. Standing at the threshold, they go only but so far. Her hands behind his head his arms around her waist. Lips slow moving penetrating each other's spirit.

Wanting the experience of living in each other's body, this moment in time is secured with a mutual pause. Neither ask why the other chose to stop they just share a look then a swallow. They have every reason for yes but not now the only answer now is not the time.

On the other side of town we find Derik at one of those moments after a game when he walks into his apartment dropping the ball on the beanbag chair and trying to let go of thoughts of his insecurities over Christopher and Mysary. Pick up games with friends on the court allow a momentary escape from dealing with personal issues. In the calm down time after the game, the boys talk but nothing too deep. After three and a half almost four years, you would think things would be settled in his mind. Hell you would think after four years it would be a none-issue but it has only grown and rather than address the thoughts that linger, Derik just allows them to fester. He tries to over compensate by outward romantic forms of expression. Checking the time, he jumps in the shower washing away the day as each and every bead of sweat is ripped from his frame and tossed down the drain. Now dressed, he is thinking how long it would take to get to the station and wondering if there is anything he forgot. Sure to spritz on her favorite Eternity for Men last so that it endures all the way up to Liberty Heights. Grabbing all the essentials, checking his watch realizing he only has about 12 minutes to reach the train station and get set up. He's off.

Derik has tried to get beyond the fact that Christopher and Mysary are best friends. The jealousy never really wears off it just becomes a little less of a burden. In the early days of the relationship, she would often talk to Derik about Christopher. Not in a way that you would assume they were together. Mysary saw it as if it was my girlfriend and I talked about it, it wouldn't be a problem so why would it be a problem if it were Chris. The best way to explain this moment is like this. Derik tries to battle personal inadequacies with a slew of memorable moments in an effort to create a better foundation for the two of them. The fact is that he will never be the one she runs to for everything. He knows Mysary luvs him and the fact that he has resisted the temptation to go all the way speaks volumes about his commitment to their relationship. They have grown so close; most people wonder if they are married. The thorn in this rose is that ever since he found out Christopher and Miz have a deep and close bond that goes beyond the physical is a problem. The thought that another man has something he could never have sometimes tears him apart. So today Derik takes the time to recreate a small moment from one of Miz's favorite movies. Knowing her schedule, he waits until she walks from the train to her car coming up behind he says...

Derik: [13]I have crossed oceans of time to find you.

Recognizing his voice and the soft drift of his cologne she releases her pepper spray. Turning around slow she asks

Miz: What did you say?

Derik: I said, " I have crossed oceans of time to find you."

It's like all the stress of the day melted with just that one line. How does he do it? You want to ask. Why, if he feels it will never release him from believing she will truly be his some day. Is he a gluten for punishment? Is this some sort of game one on one with individual perception? Is it even fair? The luv of the moment is held hostage and pimped to create with the intent to suppress defeated thoughts.

Miz: Derik, really what are you doing here? I mean I am glad you are here but this is unexpected.

Derik: Well I can't really say why I just wanted to do something nice. I had this feeling you needed me. So, come with me.

Miz: Where are we going? I really want to …

A small picnic was laid out in the area near the parking lot with sparkling cider, a little raspberry brie, and fresh chilled fruit. This

---

[13] This is a line from Brahm Stoker's Dracula. Mysary's favorite movie

131

simple arrangement, the careful thought and execution continues to warm her heart. These little things to justify his love build a case for Mysary to give in to the fact that Derik is the man she needs and wants. She has spent a portion of their relationship emotionally tied to an affair with Christopher, now is the time to let it go. Focusing on the here and now is the best way to do so. Say what you want, she is only into Derik more because Chris has found someone who poses a real threat to her friendship. They enjoy a nice picnic and good conversation. While the world rushes home around them they breathe.

Miz: Mmm. This is good. Where did you get it?

Derik: You want the romantic lie or the crazy truth.

Miz: The truth doesn't start with you rolling in a doughnut does it?

Derik: Who told you? Aw I might as well spill the beans. Really though, I got the recipe from Publix.

Miz: You mean to tell me this is a Derik hands on creation? I'm impressed. So what do you have planned for an encore?

Derik: Wouldn't you like to know?

Miz: I asked didn't I?

Derik: So let me ask you something?

Miz: Drastically changing the topic.

Derik: Seriously, did you ever think we would be together this long?

Miz: I never put a time limit on things. Why? How long did you think we would last?

Derik: I don't know. There were sometimes when I knew it was a wrap.

Miz: Example?

Derik: There were just those times when I wasn't sure how you felt about me. The only other relationship that I was in that showed some promise ended really badly. I didn't want to make those mistakes with you and I didn't want to make comparisons you know?

Miz: I am beginning to see. Derik, are you okay?

Derik looking off a little not really sure how to say what is on his heart, so he digresses. Mysary can see and is sure she knows what it is, but until he says something she will let him continue with the self-inflicted suffering. Just then here phone rings.

Chris: Hey, you busy?

Miz: (*More concerned about Derik at the moment she doesn't recognize the tone she takes with him*) Kind of. What do you want?

Christopher bothered by the tone just says never mind, later, then hangs up. You would think that Mysary's next statement would allude to something else but, well you be the judge on what is really being said.

Miz: Hey, you want to take this back to your place so we can talk some more there?

Derik: Nah, It'll keep.

Miz: Well, if you're sure? It's getting a little late and I have to get an early start on tomorrow …

Helping her up from the blanket, Derik walks Mysary to her truck after they pack up and load his car. It appears that now, affections are reciprocated in public a little more than usual. Almost as if Derik has his heart on his sleeve and Mysary could somehow read the writing. Maybe it's love revealing itself consistently after so many years and this is the epiphany of recognition. What would make him stay if it isn't the sex and up until now the constant rejection to the idea of public signs of affection? Whatever it is it feels both great and confusing simultaneously. We try to avoid the fact that within us is a burning need to be wanted; this idea is usually hidden behind mounds of personal baggage or the aftermath of a relationship. Truthfully speaking, it is easier to let go of the pain of the past but somehow the bruises are always in fashion and it cost too much to change styles.

Mysary and Derik kiss, then say their goodbyes, both feeling better about the day now that they ended the day together. Mysary on the way home spends the time reflecting on how much she really luvs Derik and why she waisted so much time playing games with him. A fifteen

134

minute drive home seems to go on forever when you are deep in thought and the songs on the radio plays to your every emotion like some cruel joke. Myasry has been tabling the thought of what to do about the job offer or grad school in town. Her decision is a little clearer or at least for the moment the scale is tilted. Derik is now pondering if he is ready to go all the way with his confession of luv. A virgin to the thought of how to pop the question after having never seen love in real life, he wonders if this is the time.

Hoping to get home to maybe finally talk to Airicka about things she is quickly disappointed her car is not there. Secretly she is praying that Chris would be home. She calls him back but it goes directly to voice mail then opening the door, Mysary is alone. Derik texts that he is home and that he hopes she had a good time. Replying had a great time and TTYL (Talk To You Later). The question now is does she text Chris to find out where he is. Mysary is still unaware of Mai Luv and how much Chris is really into her. What was his call to her about? She sends a text to Chris that she is free now. He doesn't respond.

As a sign of some level of trust, Mai gives Chris the keys to her car preferring that he drive and also affirming his role in the relationship as the man. She didn't question why he was without a car. Chris told her he was putting money aside for graduate school. It would have been easy to think he was just like every other guys she's known in the past except going to the bank with him and watching how he manages his finances put any doubt to rest. Christopher never took advantage of her trust he just uses the car as an opportunity to prove that everything to this point has been nothing but the truth.

No matter how shallow or deep a relationship is, there are always tests to see how serious one maybe. So she may look to see if you will open the door for her every time whether coming or going. He looks to see if she unlocks his door from the inside. You both agree that friendship is important and nothing should get in the way of that. It's amazing here the both of you view the word friend the same.

Just a casual Saturday out begins with the art museum and then a trip to Old Town for window-shopping which leads to a stop at a coffee shop or a smoothie shop. Maya is very attractive and every time they kiss even just the simplest of greetings it's like an explosion of hormones. Unlike any other woman in his life; his vow of purity is put through a serious test. So Christopher has taken the time to plan outings to avoid those temptations. Maya unaware of his plans just takes the time to enjoy their time together.

Mai: I never realized there was so much to do here.

Chris: Yeah the movies thing is so played. Sam and I used to hit the "[14]*Loaf*" every Wednesday to do something different on the weekend.

Mai: I learn more and more about you. Hmmm, so you just the new age brother huh? Poetry, singing, no kids, straight, and good credit. You do have okay credit?

Chris: You know now that school is over I got that grace period before the big payback.

---

[14] The Loaf is local newspaper filled with events and happenings

Mai: So how is it up there?

Chris: The weather's nice in summer. How are the winters on Venus?

Mai: Good, you gotta see me in my bunny suit.

With a wrinkle of her nose and soft lick of her lips, she smiles with a seductive innocence. He closes his eyes and says...

Chris: Wow.

Chris now stops mid thought with a look that shows an emotion that can't really be explained. Mai puzzled by the look does what any person would do, she asks.

Mai: What?

Chris: Just thinking of a how much I never liked bunnies until just now.

Mai: Really, Why is that?

Chris: You are kidding me right? I mean honestly you have to know how fine you are.

Mai: No, tell me.

Chris: Girl, you're bout as fine as a big plate of lawd hamercy with a side of thank you Jesus. Seriously though, all jokes aside. You're beautiful.

Maya Luvs, being coy doesn't respond with laughter or anything. She simply says

Mai: I see

Chris: So it's like that?

Mai: Like what? What are you talking about?

Chris: The "I see" just seems to be a little hard to interpret.

Mai: Oh.

Chris: You weren't offended by what I said were you?

Mai: No, should I have been?

Noticing the comment but certain not to respond with the typical what has never been her style. If someone wants to give the information, cool if not then she'll wait until they are less guarded. Chris still baffled by her unpredictable nature continues...

Chris: No one has really approached a conversation with me the way you do. Most people turn and run when I want to talk. They say I make their brains hurt. You, you're different. I don't know what it is but I like it a lot.

Mai: Well I am glad we reached this plateau in our relationship. So what want or need was filled here?

Chris: Well to be truthful…

Mai: As I hope you would be.

Chris: There has always been a need in me to find someone to talk to. I mean really share some of my thoughts with stupid and serious.

Mai: Oh come on, you kidding me right? You don't seem like the type to have a shortage of friends.

Chris: Yeah, I have friends but I was looking for someone who wouldn't be so easy to figure out. I get tired of people who get caught up in what I do in the relationship instead of trying to be an equal part. They never really seem interested in the way my mind works or they are intimidated but how fast it moves. So eventually I figure a way to have fun. I manipulate the environment to suit my needs until I have no more use for them.

Mai: So what's to say you won't get bored with me? Will I become just another captured queen in this mental game of chess you enjoy.

Chris: I don't know what the future holds. Right now I am really feeling you. And that's not because I haven't been in a relationship of substance since sophomore year.

Mai: So what happened? I mean if that's not prying too deep.

Chris: You kidding me right? After you poured yourself out to me when you did, please. This is me paying what I owe. She was a year a head of me and I was working part-time at this sub shop. I had seen her around campus a few times and it was usually with her boyfriend. You would have thought the two of them were never going to part ways.

Mai: Why you say that?

Chris: This dude went and had his Mustang GT painted pink because it was her favorite color. I mean if that don't say something I don't know what will. How are you going to look rollin through town in a pink Mustang GT? What was bananas was when word got out that the two of them broke up, dudes and some girls started pushing up on her like an exercise while he became one of the biggest jokes of the year.

Mai: Not you right? (*With a hint of sarcasim*)

Chris: Really as much as I wanted to, our paths never crossed until she started coming by the sub shop on Sunday morning before work. We started talking, went out to dinner a few times and really hit it off.

Mai: So what made it so cool?

Chris: For me it was the fact that we could do crazy stuff like drive out to the mountains and play Scrabble. She wasn't afraid to bust out a coupon. Not that I was a cheap scape, it was cool to know she was down.

Mai: Wait. Did you say Scrabble?

Chris: Yeah we would do all kinds of silly things. There was no pressure on either side. We just enjoyed being together.

Mai: Now its time for the million dollar question.

Chris: Why we're not together anymore. Well I guess as time went on she thought she could change me. My friends namingly the two I live with. She voiced her opinion often about how she felt uncomfortable with Miz and Airicka. It got to the point where I just had to tell her these are my friends and you could like it or lump it. I'm with you not them.

Mai: Let me ask you something then? You don't feel like her request was too much to ask at least to try and save the relationship?

Chris: Well that's hard to answer with a straight yes or no, as much as it pained me to do it I had to. I mean Miz and I have been friends since way back and Airicka had been around since the summer of freshman year. We never tried any hook up or any of that secret friendship stuff. We are just roommates who are friends, besides with my job, the group, school, and her not in that order, but who had time for anything else? I really felt like she didn't trust me so we went our separate ways.

Mai: Do you ever regret your decision?

Chris: You may find this a little harsh but I don't believe in regrets. Whatever decision I make I live with it.

Mai: Why is that?

Chris: Regrets are nothing but a waist of time. I mean, what can regret do to change the decision or the pending outcome? Anyone not satisfied with the results of their own choice didn't at least entertain the thought of the possible scenario and that's why they are unhappy.

Mai: You're right that is a little harsh. So who was she? That hurt you so bad you built the protective wall around yourself.

Chris: Nobody. I expect people to be people that way there is no pressure of being let down or disappointed.

Mai: So let me ask you this then, what do you want to come of us? You said you were looking for someone to talk to. What about your roommates you could never talk to them?

This question is two-fold in that it gives information requested on the surface but also a look into the possible competition or threat. Chris so quick to catch the plow openly divulges information.

Chris: We talk, but there are some things you would like to share with someone closer than a friend. They have their relationships and sometimes they are not available.

Mai: Humph. So what about us? Oh, remember flattery will get you almost anywhere.

Chris: Almost anywhere? Um.

Mai: I'm no push over, that cute thing will only get you to a point,

142

mister.

Chris: Well then, good for you.

Mai: Really? Why you say that?

Chris: Because now you get to benefit from (short pause) Me.

Mai: Oh my, we are confident aren't we?

Chris: This you better believe.

Mai: Yeah I bet you say that to all the girls. But back to what we were talking about.

And this is how it happens, without warning or signs of danger ahead but with a simple question.

Chris: Sure.

Mai: Why me?

Chris: Huh?

Mai: Why me?

Chris: Why you what?

Mai: Seriously, why are you so into me? It's only been a few months.

143

What makes me so different that you want to be with me?

Chris: You serious?

Mai: Yeah, I want to know?

Chris: What do you really want to know?

Mai: What do you mean?

Chris: Why are you asking me this now out of the clear blue?

Mai: Not out of the blue, Chris. I mean we have been seeing each other for a while now and I just want to know what "THIS" is. What we are?

Chris: So this is about titles or labels?

Mai: No, I would like to know how you see me or should I say us?

Chris: Okay, now you asking me something different?

Mai: How is this different?

Chris: First you asked me why you. Now you ask me to define us. So which is it?

Mai: Forget it.

Chris: Why are you mad?

Mai: I'm not mad.

Chris: You sure look and sound like it?

Mai: Whatever. It doesn't matter?

Chris: If it didn't matter then why did you ask it?

Mai: Just drop it ok?

Chris: I don't get this.

Mai: What?

Chris: Nothing.

And just like that a battle begins, silence. Everyone has been here before and you can go back and forth on who is right or wrong but it doesn't change the situation at all. There needs to be a resolution.

Chris: Ok look, apparently something I said upset you. I don't want to go mess up what I feel is a very good time. So can we please start over?

Mai: No, no we can't.

A little thrown by her words.

Mai: Well we can't start over with out Keno, the park and your sexy pancake poem. Besides I just got my hair done and I'm not running anywhere to mess this up.

Chris: Good one.

Mai: Thank you. Thank you, I will be here all week.

Chris: So we are good?

Mai: Yeah it's good.

Chris: Word, just like that?

Mai: Why, harp on what I can't change and I am having a good time as well.

As simple as a well placed joke, crisis is averted. They can now continue the conversation under reasonable means. Seeing that Christopher never had any ill intent Maya, was having a great time. An argument over miscommunication could easily be resolved when one person is willing to take a step back from their point and let it go. Truthfully speaking, could you have avoided a fight or two if you?

Derik and Mysary have gone out before but tonight was different. There is a change in the air, neither can see it coming though.

Derik: I was thinking, I got some time off coming up. What if we flew to Virginia and checked things out? You know places to live and shop.

146

Mysary: Oh so you think you can sweep me off to another state for the weekend, take me shopping, and well what exactly?

Derik: I don't think you understand what I am asking.

Mysary: Then what are you asking?

Derik: Well I know you didn't really like the pressure of trying to decide to stay or go. So I looked into transferring to Virginia , and I thought we could work at making us a little more permanent.

Mysary: I know you mean well (*Before continuing she cuddles his face and kisses him gently.*) The two of us in a city where we only know each other would be hard. I know we've been together for a while now but I think it's too soon to move in together.

Calculating her next step trying still to lighten the rejection

Mysary: Now if you want to go away to take me shopping I'm game for that. (*Kissing him again, this time a little more with the intent..*)

Derik allows the pain to subside while Mysary masters the art of escapism once again. The issue is not resolved like many things in their relationship; it is put aside until later when it will resurface is a good question.

Being at Mai's house so much Chris has started making dinner from time to time and helped Mai's sister with her homework. On their days off mostly the weekend before the band has to play, the three of them spend time around town. The game ranch seems to be the favorite, a place where the summer heat is blocked by the shade and the joy of feeding the animals. It is so much fun you forget how hot you are. Or if there is an activity going on at the art museum, Mai is quick to make the plans for a day trip. She is always sure to get some great pictures for her photo album. Most times the day is not complete without a visit to the Chart House, the Rusty Skupper, or one of the spots downtown where the three of them grab a bite to eat enjoying life. They look like a ready-made family but for now, Chris seems to be just visiting their lives with the option to stay. It happens to be an ordinary night at Mai's home. Chris is sitting in the living room playing a game with Mai's sister before bedtime.

Chris: (*calls to Mai*) Hey could you bring me a glass of tea?

Mai: Sure, would his highness care for anything else.

Chris: A full plate of you would be nice.

Mai coming in the living room glass in hand

Mai: I didn't catch that last part

Chris: Huh? … Uh … I said how bout stew and chicken fight.
Mai: Right. You can't lie good at all. You better not ever get into politics. So what did you really say?

Not ready to open that can of worms Christopher just continues on.

Chris: Hmm. That sounds like a pretty good idea. I mean I do have a strong public servant background.

Mai: Yes, your demographic is what again? 3rd through 6th graders.

Chris: Right.

Mai: You know if you choose to go that route I got your back.

Chris: Nice to know, better to hear.

Mai, collapses on the sofa on the opposite side of Chris. With a deep breath she sends her sister to bed. Of course, as all siblings do, simple negotiations for a few more minutes are the immediate form of resistance. Noticing Mai's unwillingness to fight, Chris steps in and offers to read a bed time story if she gets ready for bed in 15 minutes. Like a track star she accomplishes the goal and calls down to Chris when she is ready.

Mai: You don't have to

Chris: Relax babe. I'll be back in a minute.

Going upstairs Chris tucks her in and looking at the book she has ready, begins to read The Giving Tree. His voice and the repetition of the book send the little listener to a sweet sleep. Not taking any chances, Chris finishes the story before leaving. Turning off the light he's back downstairs to where Mai is curled up on the sofa looking around the room he finds a panda brown throw folded in a chair.

Covering her completely, turning off the TV, and then calls Sam to come pick him up. Sam, living not far and probably just getting off work, says no problem. Within15 minutes Sam pulls up to the house beeping the horn once Chris gently kissing her on the head grabs his coat and leaves.

Chris: Thanx dude.

Sam: No problem (*as he yawns*).

Chris: I guess my powers worked too well tonight. They both went to sleep.

Sam: I thought I told you about laying the smack down on the food and stuff.

Chris: (*Stroking his mustache slow*) Well you know, what can I say?

Sam: So you never told me what Miz thinks of your new honey.

Chris: We haven't had a chance to talk about it really, since that night at Shelia's.

Sam: Oh yeah I forgot about that night. Ya'll havent talked since then what's really going on?

Chris: Nothing.

Sam: Riiight. I believe that.

Chris: Whatever dude.

Just then the piano track to Chris'[15] new song comes on through the speakers. They both jump in on the parts of the song where the harmony has needed some work.

· **Chris & Sam:** ♫ ♪Let's get back to love, Stay with me what we have cannot end...

Sam: ...♫ ♪Because I can't go on with
Chris: Nah, see the problem is that those lines are supposed to overlap almost.

Sam: Like this. ♫ ♪because i can't go on without you,

Chris: ♫ ♪You maybe in another town♫ ♪

Sam: Okay so we all sing the lets get back to love and you come back in off the solo line with stay with me?

Chris: Yeah that's it. The harmony is great but that timing is everything for this song.

Sam: Which reminds me, I have been meaning to ask you about this song. Where did this one come from?

Chris: It started with the hook and then went from there.

---

[15] Play Track Without You (instrumental)

151

Sam: That's not what I meant. What's the first line?

Chris: (*not really understanding where this is going*) Thinking back on you and me remembering the way things used to be.

Sam: and that line doesn't mean anything?

Chris: What do you mean?

Sam: Nothing man nothing.

Chris: Is Tischa spying through you again?

Sam: When is she not?

On the way to Chris' house they trip out hard on the sights and the events of the last band rehearsal and how they imagine the concert will go. From time to time, serious issues are brought to the front of the conversation but they are dealt with in the usual manner and then it's back to the land of 1,000 laughs. Chris as the constant inquisitor is balanced by the quick snappy wit of Sam. It's friendships like these that keep men grounded and at the very least provides you with a foxhole partner.

Chris: …Nah fool, remember when you tried to hook up with that sleestack at the Foxe's Den. And you can't blame it on the alcohol either.

Sam: You ain't gonna never let a brother live that down, are you?

Christopher throwing his arms in the air like some wild monsters backing it up with ghostly moans to the point of uncontrolled laughter. Sam trying to ignore the taunts can't help but laugh too. An almost breathless Christopher

Chris: Wait, wait, "♫ ♪in the laaaand aannd of the lost♫ ♪"

Sam: You done.

Chris: Whoah I needed that.

Sam: So yo Tischa is bugging about how we haven't been out in a while.

Chris: Well Mai, is taking care of her younger sister, so most of what we do involves her.

Sam: How old is she?

Chris: Eight.

Sam: Shit, you had me thinking she was like four or five. Hell, bring her along too, anything, to get T off my back about this.

Chris: Alright I'll talk to her about it.

Sam: So what's the deal is she Venny material or the Mereka type?

Chris: Wha... Why?

153

Sam: Well I need to know if she will be a part of the choir of women you eventually dump and remain friends with. You know I plan to bring them all together on your actual wedding day. Dress them up in red and have them singing "Congratulations"[16] as a gift to you or is she a possible.

Chris: You make it sound like I've been with a gang a women

Sam: Let's see there's Mireka, Chrissy, Nicole, Myesha, Tasha. Tischa, Prantika, Charon oh and how could I forget Donna. Don't get me started on the other 3 and a half plus years of on again off again on again with Ms. ...

Chris: ...A'ight don't go there. They never overlapped and I never left one for another, unlike some people.

Sam: Yeah I know. You the only brotha I know who can break up with a girl and still be her friend. How do you do it? It's that virginity thing ain't it? Come clean Chris, it's got to be the virginity thing.

Chris: It is what it is. On the real though, don't get it twisted there have been those moments when all I wanted was to hit the skins.

Sam: How you sound hit the skins? What are you 12 again? Who says that anymore? Next thing you gonna sing Knockin' Boots. Can a brotha get a modern day reference?

---

[16] Youtube search "Congratulations" Vesta if you don't understand

154

Creatively silent for the moment a witty comeback brews, Chris patiently waits for that opportune time.

Sam: What? You got nothing to say? I realize that your women are all sprung on that voice and virginity thing so they let the corny songs mess slide but I won't. I can't. What kind of friend would I be if I didn't clown you. Don't get mad at me for calling it out bruh.

Chris: OOooh this love is sooo, um that I won't let you go. (Al B. Sure) That was the song you sang right? You did have on that silver suit and one black pleather glove, and I do believe the grind made its way into that performance.

Sam: You so stupid, where the hell you pull that one from?

Chris: ACTSO Talent show you do remember?

Sam: Why a brotha gotta bring up the past umph, umph?

Chris: You just remember I still got the tape and if you don't want it all over Youtube you will breeze back with the comments.

Sam: Don't think I forgot what we were talking about. You and I both know they are just hoping to be the one. That's the only reason why they're hanging around calling every so often, to see how you doing. They are crowding you like sharks waiting for blood in the water.

Chris: There you go. Women ain't all about the physical and neither am I.

[Ok to you the reader of this, I am lying my ass off. It is not easy trying to hold on to my virginity. Why are you women so beautiful? Oh my ever loving GOD!] There have been just some really good people I have met and I thought it could be something.

Sam: For real C, I know you want me to believe that, but people are people and we are sexual beings. Not that we are driven by sex but attraction goes two ways you ain't like most other dudes out there. I could see how you made it through high school but four years of college and singing with a band, that ain't regular. Then the fact that you keep a good relationship after you split up is crazy. Who does that? I mean you help them hang up Christmas lights, their mom's be treatin' you like family, letting you sleep in their house. Who does that? Come on what guy you know gets that treatment even when they are still with the Shorty?

Chris: Yo, How'd we get way over here on this? I'm trying to tell you about Maya and you still stuck slanging old stuff like I'm a relationship ho or something.

Sam: My bad, go on, tell me how she's different than the rest of them. Y'all connect on some metaphysical level. She's the sugar to your red kool-aid.

Chris: On the up and up she's hot man. All jokes aside it's something cool about her.

To make it plain Mai Luv has some how done what no other woman has ever been able to do. She has kidnapped Christopher's heart.

156

Sam: So when do we really get to meet her. I mean if she comes to the show Saturday will we all go to Copeland's after. Is she the type you take to Copeland's with your people?

Chris: Yeah dude, that's what's up. We can shut it down like last time. I will talk to her about it and see what she says. It should be cool.

Sam: So what has Miz said about this one?

Christopher now quiet as if speaking about this new found luv interest is taboo. The fact is that he has tried to talk to his best friend for a few weeks now but their schedules never seem to align themselves with the opportunity for conversation. They talk on the phone via text about what is needed for the house but neither has really had the chance to catch the other one up on the latest since graduation. Sam picking up on the silence

Sam: Why you get silent all of a sudden? You haven't told Mysary have you? Wow, this one must be something you ain't told your home girl. Are you finally moving on?...

The question comes just as they reach the house. No lights are on although Miz's truck is in the driveway. Sam and Christopher dap it up.

Christopher: Yo, See you Saturday.

Sam: Dude, don't think I forgot about it.

Throwing up the deuces the conversation ends at that moment. Chris

157

goes in the house, walking upstairs to his room. It's apparent everyone was sleeps or just not at home. Turning on the iPod, Chris crashes too.

Its Saturday, Sheila's Café is the local spot where the neo soul community comes to fellowship. Each wall is its own collage of abstract expressionism painting and far beyond conventional statues guides the flow and feel. The butter soft blue and sweet red lights seem to ignite small areas of cozy at each individual table as the brick and hard wood floors carry a breeze of meditation and honey through out this two level sanctuary. The place looks nothing like it did graduation night. The downstairs is a haven to one of the most dynamic restaurants and juice bars in the city. The upstairs is a relaxed venue of entertainment. Poets, interpretive dancer, psalmist and singers all gather here express the beauty form and creativity. Tonight and for the past few Saturdays UNiTY is the feature. Just before they go on, a local comedian takes the stage to a subtle array of applause.

B4 Real: What up people? I said what up people?!? All the ladies, all the ladies, all the ladies in the house say hey! A'ight for those who don't know, I am B4 Real. No seriously that's my name. I don't have a lot of time up here so let's jump right into it. Yo, I gosta tell the truth here.

Audience: BE FOR REAL! (*those that have seen him know that is a part of the routine*)

B4 Real: Fa real. Fa Real. I need Jesus. Check this out I went to this one church. I should have known something was wrong when the sign on the front was written on cardboard and in airbrush letters. No lie

Blessed Church & Check Cashin'. I know what you thinking, be for real, I am. So I went in 'cause you know how hard it is to find a good check cashin place that don't want fity leven percent. But that aint it at all, the pastor had on this crème and orange linen suit and smellin all like ginseng and Viagra. He started with the offering! Clearing his voice and now with that southern twang he says. Now I knowt dat y'all be thinking the passa tryin' ta how they say getcha ta give up the goods but i'ma splaint taya how we give unta the Lawd. Ya see at dem dere white churches dey collects the offerin' den draw a circle on the flo and the precha takes the money and throws it in the air. Whatever lands in the circa goes to God and what lands outside goes to the church. We here at the Greater Blessed Baptist Temple and check cashin' knowt aint no circa big enough fo God. So when we collect da offerin' we too throws it in the air, whatever stays there belongs to God...

The laughter so hot it overruns the end of the joke.

B4 Real: ...Yo I can't make this stuff up. Nah but on the serious tip though, my grandfather was a wise man. I remember some of the soundest advice he ever gave me. He looks me square in the face and said, "Look here boy I'm going to share some wisdom with ya. And if you hold tight to it you'll be a wealthy man. Now let me ask you a question. How do you reuse a rubber? When you're finished you take it off and shake the FUCK out of it"...

Once again the gut busting laughter is so huge that his thank you is drowned by the ovation from everyone in the club. Being so well received he prepares to bring on the band letting the people know he'll be back during the break in sets. The band doesn't need much to set up

159

and now Christopher takes center stage to a rush of whistles and applause.

Christopher: Thank you, thank you. Let's hear it again for B4 Real... YO, we just found out B will performing at the Realto and the Myerhoff. So y'all just got a taste of what it's going to be like. B has some flyers and tickets if you're interested. How much are they?

B4 Real: (*shouting from the audience*) $15.00 for one $25.00 for two.

Chris: Thas' what's up make sure you check it out. And as you already know we are UNiTY and we are glad to be here to perform some new things we have been working on and some of your faves. We hope you enjoy.

After the count off the band plays as Chris marinates the rhythm with his scat. To a packed house the band transitions into their first song a duet with bassist Tischa.
♫ ♪So in Luv With You
As the night falls to an end
And the sun lays across your chin
Slowly from a sleep we rise
With a kiss that rains butterflies ♫ ♪
in spring so in Luv With You...

The song quickly becomes one of the crowd favorites as the band plays the hook softly to the continued movement of the crowd. Just as the snare starts the rhythm it closes out the tune as Chris begins.

160

Christopher: Thank you, so we're going to flip things a little.

Lady in the crowd: Do what you want baby, do what you want.

Scattered light-hearted laughter as some of the other single ladies in the crowd quietly agree. Chris always moved by the sentiment responds in kind with a smile. Seizing the moment the band begins to play this really sexy melody

Chris: Ok, to all the women who wanted to say that and especially to the one who took a chance, here is a special number we have been working on. It was originally intended for someone very special to me but I realize you all came to hear us so this one is to all the ladies who continue to support.

The men in the audience take different approaches to this. More than half are nodding with the word or that's what's up. But there are some who are sprinkled around with the something stinks around here look on their faces and are simply hating because, well who cares about them damn haters. If you don't have someone hating on you then you must not be living up to your possibilities. Chris turning to the band a soft sound of the snare ripples across the air followed by the hypnotic massage of piano keys ringing a sweet melody. Many of the ladies in the crowd smile. Some who know Miz glance in her direction.

Janet: Umph, I wonder who he could be singing about. I guess it is good that it just so happens that Derik couldn't make it tonight.

Looking a little moved by the sentiment but not enough to let those

161

watching know the candlelight's reflection in her eyes shimmers as a
tear pools. Cut quick by the comments of one, Mysary begins to throw a
look that kills fast and quick. Before the thought could manifest Neecie
interjects with a stern look that says girl don't go there. Fading from
the shadows into the blue lights of the stage his lips bless the mic.

Christopher:

♫ ♪Girl, I want to let you know

Since the day I met you I know

We've been, wanting the same thing

You don't have to worry about the time we lost

The games we played with other lovers

The rest of now starts with us

Hold on baby, to my every word no games of chance

My love is here for you trust.

There is something about you

When you let me hold you I can tell we are meant to be

I know you feel it, look at me! ♫ ♪

Everyone in the audience stops as the command in voice, how it bares
the style of Teddy Pendergrass and Marvin Gaye in one breath. The
sexiness of it drives the next line home and an orgasmic chill up and
the spine of the women.

Christopher: Tell me you don't agree.

UNiTY: ♫ ♪Oh how I need you to fall

       With me baby

       This is all or nothing

162

And I'm all in how about you... ♫ ♪

Fading the music first then scats drift behind, the air is filled with smiles and glossy eyes on luvrs and others.

Toni: Ooo, Lord child ump, ump. Ump! And he can sing.

Kia: Aw that was so sweet did he write that for you Miz?

Even the strong prison of stoicism couldn't withstand this attack. Her walls fell to pieces like soft ice cream cones. But assuredly she could not let the others see this moment of imperfection. Slowly exhaling she turns back to the table where the girls are all stares and smiles. Back to the stage the band prepares to break. Gently swaying through the speakers under the stroke of Chris's voice the DJ Spins "Be Sweet on Me" His eyes possess the crowd for that one single solitary moment even the kiss of fluttered hearts is stilled to a hush. Soft lips dance on straws, twirled ice on rings like crystal tears but one pair of hands cradle a shifting head alone at the table her eyes strike back with a quiet riot. I'm right here and like a hook his subtle slow turn confirmed recognition.

Chris: We'll be right back in a moment to finish this set. Let's keep this business growing, your waiters and waitresses are here to serve you. While you get your drink on let's give it up again for B4 Real Thank you.

As Chris and the band leave the stage the house music picks up where the mood left off. The staff is taking orders in large amounts. Chris

163

walks through the crowd as the house lights come up from dark to dim. There are lighted-hearted praise, daps, flirtatious winking eyes, and smiles seem to shower him. Drawing closer to Miz's table inconsistent eye contact is made and lost. Chris making a quick left at last sight Mysary wonders where he went. She can never give in to the fact she was waiting for him to show so she plays it off before anyone could catch on. Christopher now stands at a small table in the corner where Mai is draped with some unpleasant company. DeyShawn and the blessed scent of "Our version of High Karate" over powers the meditation candle set as the centerpiece.

DeyShawn: Yo mommy, so wha's the deal? You kickin the digits or what?

Of course with a stern intercession Chris responds to the look of distress in Mai's eyes.

Chris: Yo son, she with me.

DeyShawn: Dawg, my bad. But you can't be leavin a dime like this unattended. Pockets get picked fast.

On the sly, trying to catch her eye as he leaves the table you know how it's done.

Christopher: On the real, just bounce.

Muttered words under punkified breath are uttered "I should fly that head, punk". But they aren't even entertained more important matters need attention.

Mai: Hey you.

Mai: It was cool. You know that bass player was kind of throwing down. The whole band played nice. (*Smiling at the mental game of cat and mouse)*Oh yeah, that last song was sweet.

Christopher: Oh you got jokes. Taking her by the hand. Come with me before I have to go back up.

Mai: You aint tryin to take me to meet your parents are you?

Christopher: Nah, some of my people I want you to meet.

Guiding her through the darkness she pulls closer for more than one reason. The first to avail at the table from the shadows all eyes turn and light up as his frame stands firm against the dark. Mysary turns and smiles gently.

Chris: Ladies. Hope all is well.

Janet: Hey. Now that you're here it just got better.

Cheesing and grinning almost certain to sit with her 28 D's in plain view. Mysary cuts her eyes as if to say you got one more chance to mess with me. Interrupting the moment ...

Chris: Miz, I haven't had the opportunity to talk to you in the past few weeks, there is someone I'd like to meet. Mysary LeNoir everybody I'd like you to meet Mai Luv.

There is nothing in twenty-seven languages, fifty dialects, and more than two hundred clichés could explain the scene of disgruntled silence that had befallen this small area. Totally oblivious to the mood shift he continues pointing out each person identifying them one by one.

Chris: Mai this is Kia, Toni, Coco, Janet, Neecie and my best friend for as long as I can remember, Mysary Le Noir.

As eyes cut and castrate in utter disapproval, with apprehension and a subtle charm, Mai bares the weight of this pressure and with an innocent smile responds.

Mai: Hello, nice to meet you, Chris I need to freshen up I'll be back.

Chris: Okay.

Leaning in for a kiss on the check, modestly and respectfully she shuns the advance and walks off. Mysary stands beside Chris and utters softly.

Miz: How long have you known her and already givin' pet names? Is that how you carryin' it now?

No one but Chris and Neecie notice the cynical undertone in her voice; Chris playing it off mildly, but his response is quick and precise.

Chris: That's her name. (*Leaning in closer to her*) As if you cared anyway.

Neecie catches a hint of the pain in Mysary's face. Like any champion thought she covers it with a nonchalantness. Whatever Chris said. Neecie knows this calls for immediate rescue procedures.

Neecie: Hey girl, come with me I need to ask you something, we'll be back.

Chris: I'll talk to you after the set.

With stale looks continuing from the remaining members of the table as quickly as he came even quicker he leaves. Now on their way to the ladies room Miz and Neecie enter as Mai comes out. Exchanged looks from "You @#!" to "Your looks don't faze me" pass as no words are said. Meeting up with Chris, Mai looks at her watch.*

Mai: Hey you, it's a little later than expected and I've got an early day tomorrow. Chris's face sinks into a small but sullen state with the news. The power of a woman's words and touch eases the pain of any man. Walk me to my car.

Helping her on with her coat and tells Tischa he'll be back shortly. She smiles like yeah right. In the ladies room the true nature of the situation is revealed.

Miz: What kind of, I can't believe he, just out in front of everybody, I mean who does he think he is anyway?

167

As Neecie leans into console Miz, she can only give a spirited "I know". Reaching her hands out to…

Miz: Don't Touch Me!!! Ay Dios Mio por favor ayudame! What kinda name is "My Love"! It's a joke right? Who in the hell names their child My Luv. After a deep cleansing breath Miz looks at Neecie.

Neecie: I know girl. I know.

[Mysary] Now, I know you are reading this and you are thinking the same, but really Neecie doesn't understand. I appreciate her being here for me and all but how can she know when I sure as hell don't know. For all you rational folk reading this, you're saying Derik is her man. Don't go back and reread chapter one, nothing changed you just don't have a clue. Some of you all out there know my pain, you've been there. So should I be mad? No. Can I be mad, Hell yeah! How is it justified? Don't even go there.

Walking out of the ladies room at the same time the band's interlude fades. Chris retakes the mic as Miz returns to the table. Idle gossip and chitchat is silenced.

Toni: Everything okay?

Neecie: Just let it go.

Chris looks into the crowd, even though blinded by the lights some how their eyes seem to connect. The sax and drum trap the essence of this moment without even knowing. Chris closes his eyes gently blends with the soft colored air and the mic. Then he lets loose a heart felt soulfully sad melody

Christopher: ♫ ♪Thinking back on you and me

  Remembering the way (remembering the way) it used to be

  We talk and played all through the night

  More than just surface it was something so tight

  Drying those tears chasing the pain away

  As we embrace the world just seem to fade

  For some reason we drifted this you know

  A luv like this we just can't let go

  Let's get back to us

 What we have cannot end because I can't go on WITHOUT YOU♫

Swallowed by the emotion the song's intensity rises to hook where people can't even remain seated in some cases. Mysary now marred in the middle of both a quiet pain and beautiful torture. This song for Christopher laments like an angry apology. It is no longer talent here, hearts are being served to the melody of what we all search for in old friends., The time when we remembered us. The testing of his vocal range is truly driven by passion causing a simple falling to pieces. All that matters, is the right now, this moment became like a conscious breath for the survival, the only one you would ever need. But this train wreck of scattered emotions explode like the whisper of colliding comets and all that remains are the vibrating ripples that seem to only echo the destruction.

Christopher cares for this moment as if it were the last time he would ever be with her and he molds her, he persuades her to dance with him

169

*this moment is no longer magic it is more like salvation trapped in the
eye of a hurricane and there is no protection from harm. Mysary can
only believe this is the moment she long feared, the moment that harsh
reality seduced her perfect world into surrendering. Somewhere
between just friends and best friends, a kind of love seems to happen.
Misery found company and in a moment love got in the way.*

*When the song finally ends a long ovation fills the room. Tears are
wiped away as Sheila comes to the mic.*

Sheila: Well as always this has been a great time. I want to thank you
all for coming out to support my club. Without you there would be no
Sheila's. Keep coming and tell your friends. Once again I want to
thank UNiTY for bringing it. Let's give it up one more time for
UNiTY. Now before we leave whether you are saved or not we want to
pray that you all get to your destinations safe. Chris, would you mind
closing us out in prayer?

Chris: If you would all bow your heads and focus on God. Thank you
Father for this day, before we ask you for anything we just want to say
thank you for just being God. We humbly ask that as we stand together
saved and unsaved that you watch over us all as we leave this place but
never from your awesome presence. Thank you for our friends, we love
you. We honor you in Jesus' name we pray. Amen.

*After the prayer, pretty much everyone settles up and leaves. Mysary
looks from across the nearly empty room at Christopher. Neecie stays
for support and to divert any chitchat from the girls. Nothing is said
there is confusion in their eyes. Without uttering a thing she looks at*

170

him and ask why? He equally as silent says not really sure. Neecie signaling you've been here too long girl, let's go. After the band loads the equipment and splits the money from the night, Chris, Tischa, and Sam leave together in Sam's Trooper. Sam and Tischa have dated for about five years and are to get married once they get a little more settled in their finances. Tischa has been trying to hook Chris up with one of her girlfriends. She didn't like to see him playing himself short waiting on Miz. Cruising down Greenmount Avenue they talk about the night, how well the set went then it quickly drifts to more personal matters. Everyone saw Chris with Mai so now they, mostly Tischa, wants the debriefing.

Sam: Dude, what was up with the song tonight? You put a little something extra on that.

Tischa: Was that for this new girl? I thought she left before the last set?

Sam: You know that performance will be all over the Internet by the time we get home.

Tischa: I 'm glad you ain't iggin on Miz no more.

A silence that only lasted a second but it seem to last an eternity in thought. There is a boy's unwritten code of discretion, Sam says nothing and covers any traces of awkwardness. Just as easy as men get confused in the female conversation Tischa is lost in the mix. Sam brings it back to the forefront of discussion.

171

Sam: So what's the deal son?

Chris: There is no deal yet we still in negotiation, if you know what I mean.

Sam: Oh so you haven't revealed the secret identity yet. Still mile mannered Peter Parker

Chris: You know how we do. Let me ask you a question though, how did you know when it was time? I mean when to get into the business?

Sam and Chris started the group sophomore year. Their friendship dates back to the first campus party where their mutual distaste for the contact high forced them outside. They laughed after running into each other again in church the next day, especially because the pastor's spoke about leaving the party before you catch a contact. Chris and Sam over time forged a friendship that was more like a true brotherhood. Chris trusted Sam enough to tell him what is going on and expects Sam to hold him accountable. Even with Tischa in the car there are no boundaries and Chris knows Sam will pull no punches.

Sam: Look bruh, you have waited this long, I know you are tired and this shorty may be different from the rest. But you have to know there are no take backs. You know what to do and now that you brought it up it's about to get real hot. (*Pretending to hulk up. What makes this funny is that Sam is about 125 lbs. wet*) So what you gonna do when the heat of the moment runs wild on you?

Chris: You make it sound as if I got some crippled sign on my forehead or something. I just got my priorities set. I'm just sayin I want to. Shit sticking to this Vow of Purity sucks sometime.

Sam: Yeah but on the real, falling in luv will is what hurts the most to be truthful. Anything you fall in, better believe you can fall out of. If it's that easy to fall in and out, are you really ready to risk everything you've built for it.

Tischa has been in the back seat chatting and checking messages the whole time not really paying attention to the conversation. Until she gets the idea for...

Tischa: Hey let's go out to eat after church all four of us.

Chris: Cool. Where at?

Sam: How about FoGo or Sambuca?

Tischa: Ooh yeah that will be good. We haven't been there in a long time.

Sam: There you go.

Tischa: What?

Sam: You, just want to buy a new outfit.

Tischa: Well since you brought it up I could use a new...

Sam: You see this Chris?

Chris: My name is Paul and that is between y'all.

Sam: Oh, that's jacked up bruh. You see how you leave me hanging. What is up with that?

Chris: This is grown folks biz and I learn to stay out of that stuff.

Tischa: The two of you talking like I'm not even here.

Chris: Ah shorty, you know I love you like a play cousin.

Tischa: Whatever Chris.

Pulling up to Chris', the usual goodbyes are said with the occasional joke here or there. Walking up to the door from the looks of things no one else is home yet. Quickly motoring up the stairs because like clockwork he has to go the bathroom. While in relief, keys are heard jingling at the front door, it's Airicka. She sends out a hello to attract the response from the light she sees upstairs. By the time she gets upstairs Chris is on his way out.

Airicka: What up? How did it go tonight?

Chris: Cool you know a few new faces here and there but all in all it went cool. How was work?

Airicka: It was... Where's Miz?

174

Chris: Last I saw she was off with Neecie and the crew. You know what that means.

Never bringing up the confrontation at the table and or Mai because most guys would not see what happened as something worth mentioning. And even though Christopher is not like most guys in a lot of ways he's oblivious to the thought patterns of women.

Airicka: True.

Chris: Yo, I'm off to bed. You aiight?

Airicka: Yeah.

Now you know any woman giving short one-word answers is not okay. Some may disagree with this but the truth is women in general try to draw people in to ask questions to see how much they really care. Or is it that you want to articulate what's locked away inside and you are just waiting for someone with the key to come along and let it out. There is a need for security in all facets of relationships whether it be an associate, or something deeper there is a cry to feel the strength and compassion of someone who genuinely cares. Airicka nestled in the cover of dark with her favorite book "Guess how much I love you", she meanders back downstairs to the living room for some isolated quiet time to really think on what to do. Renee's roommate moved out about a month ago so she has asked Airicka to move in. Brevin has been hanging around a little more than usual. Even though she has graduated she hasn't found a job and wonders how long before Christopher and Mysary move out. Then there is still the unresolved

175

issue with her father.

About an hour later Mysary pulls up to the house. Noticing
Christopher's light is on she gathers herself. More hurt than angry,
Mysary for the first time feels that there is break in her armor. But you
know she will never let it be known, the more unsettled she gets with
thought of what happened and what this may mean, the calmer she
becomes. Grabbing her food from Crazy John's she walks in the house
only to be halted by the words of Airicka asking how it went. Not
wanting to rehash the still fresh wounds she says in passing, it was
okay. Knowing normally when Airicka is sitting in the living room late
there is something a rye. Of course she says there is no time for my
own pain. Miz lives by the creed that if she is not there too many people
would fall. People are depended on her to be their saving grace or at
least the one to run to for advice. Even though this crazy feeling she
has about what went on tonight is in the early stages of trying to sort
itself out, the caregiver nature kicks in like it is automatic. Usually Miz
can figure out the source of the problem by what Airicka is doing. If
she sits in the window it's deep and personal and if curls up on the sofa
it usually has something to do with a relationship. Offering to share
her chicken parm, western fries, and half and half as well as that ever
present shoulder.

Miz: Hey, so how was work?

Airicka: it was…

Miz: That good huh?

Airicka: Yeah you know the routine. Brevin called to tell me he needed to talk to me about something. He sounded kind of serious.

Miz: What up with that?

Airicka: I don't know. But you know what he does to me. And Renee is getting serious, she asked me to move in with her. She says that she and Mike are through and she wants to start on us full time.

Miz: So let me ask you something? Why are you dancing between the two of them? You need to choose and be settled on it. It's unfair to use one as some sort of rebellion and the other to satisfy your unresolved daddy issues.

Now no one but Mysary could be this hard core with Airicka, well no one could do it and not be up for a serious beat down. Mysary has this uncanny ability to make us see the truth for what it is but like everything else she knows how to comfort you after the initial blow.

Miz: I love you. When have you known me to be anything other than straight with you?

Airicka: That's why I want to be like you when I grow up. You my hero placing her hands on her waist spouting the classic hero intro Dun Da nana Mysary!!!

Very quick to respond Miz looks and continues

Miz:...And her bitty from the BK Loose lips

Airicka: Why come I gotta be all that huh. Don't make me go Calisto on you.

Miz: Whatever ho…

Airicka: So tell me how was the show?

Miz pauses, as if she were immediately taken back to that moment when she met HER. The emotion never came to the surface.

Miz: It was good. The band was on point. Oh and I met Chris' new friend.

Airicka: What? When did this happen?

Miz: With Chris you can never tell.

Airicka: Ok so what is she like? When did he have the time to meet this one?

Miz: I didn't get a chance to really meet her so I can't really say too much, except she is not one from the normal pool of women he has brought up in here.

Airicka wanting to say, "Bitch please!" recognizes something wasn't right but lets it go for now. Figuring she would get more information from Mysary later. Mysary and Airicka continue to talk as they adjourn to their rooms. Airicka is the first to retire Mysary waits, looking down the hall she can see the light from Chris' room still lit.

178

Mixed emotions of anger and the desire to talk or fight, are overthrown by the emptiness she feels. Why is she feeling this way? It can't be the new girl in Chris' life; there have been many in the past. Is it the name Mai Luv or the embarrassment of being put on blast in front of everyone? What did that song mean? There are so many questions and no answers. Almost like synchronicity she goes into her room closing the door at the same time Chris comes out of his and goes into the bathroom. Looking up the hall to Miz's room for a brief moment he is a little reluctant to go and say anything. Chris has wanted to talk to Mysary about Mai and his job plans but she's been so busy with the wedding and Derik that a jealousy has found rest with him. So is Mai the current replacement luv'r to fill the void left by Mysary?

What is this thing we pretend to know that drives us? We call it love but like Cinderella in combat boots this doesn't look like the stories we were told as children. He wants to run to your rescue at the sacrifice of his ego for the embrace of your acceptance. She wants to be the beautiful woman you always encouraged. To never let the clock strike 12 on her intelligence. You're both Romeo and Juliet, your true feelings for each other missing, one another dying to have things the way they used to be. Their hearts tangle like car wreckage neither admitting fault but both wanting that friend back. What happened here? How do you call it love when you hurt this bad and it confuses you this much? Why can't it be simple? Love should be simple as a Yes or No. We are shackled to the countless number of "Maybes". Mysary and Christopher have danced around yes and no check boxes so long this is no longer love, it is comfort, and company in misery.

Maya and Christopher spend time before band rehearsal together. Not being the sick kissy, kissy boyfriend girlfriend, but cracking jokes and making plans on where to go after practice. Maya has questions about Mysary but never ask. She accepts the fact that they are friends and as long as Chris puts an effort on their relationship she is fine. They also have the occasional boyfriend girlfriend little sister tag-a-long weekend. Maya never asked Christopher to reach out to her sister, he could not see dating Maya without accepting all of her. They provide an addition to one another that they never realized they could benefit from. Maya's sister spends alternating weekends with her father providing Maya time away from being surrogate mother. Chris and Mai spend almost the entire weekend together. Friday night Chris made good on his promise of [17]Black Linguine served with a Duplin Hetteras Red (Muscadine Wine). After a beautiful dinner, they curled up on the sofa and listened to Ben Tankard and talked until they fell asleep. Before Christopher wakes up Mai goes to the bathroom for a quick brush, floss, and rinse for that good morning kiss. After officially waking up together gave Mai has this beautiful feeling of trust she can't remember having with anyone.

Chris: Good morning, beautiful.

Mai: Good morning to you handsome. (*Leaning up for a kiss. Disregarding the aroma of last night's dinner mixed with Listerine Zero.*)

Chris: (*With his hand over his mouth tongue licking his teeth.*) Hey can I brush my teeth first?

---

[17] Recipe: Black Linguine with Orange and Red Peppers (p.291)

180

Mai: Sure, you up for a little morning work out?

Chris: Ok what you talking?

Mai: Nothing much; just a little run around the reservoir.

Chris: I'm down then maybe we can go to breakfast.

Mai: You do mean after a shower right?

Chris: Yeah. I'll be near my house so I can go change, then we can hit up Double T or something. First, got to clean the breath for the good morning kiss.

Mai: You do that.

Early in the morning there are a lot of people power-walking, jogging, and strolling around the reservoir. Christopher, Maya, and Keno join the fray. They start off with a stroll and then the last quarter mile they decide (mostly Maya) to pick up the pace. Roughly 20 yards a way from where they started Maya winks at Christopher then slowly picks up speed. Taking it as a challenge but clearly outmatched gives it his best.

Mai: Well, I didn't think you would be able to keep up.

Christopher totally out of breath and bent over looks at Keno as if to say follow my lead.

Chris: I was, but I thought Keno saw a poodle. So you know I couldn't leave the pilot with out a wingman. Ain't that right dog?

Mai: Sure, if you say so.

Pulling her close, the sweat and the rush of adrenaline make this moment sexy and laughable.

Chris: Come here you. (*Wrapping arms around her.*) Oh so you think that was funny?

Mai: It was watching you hitting yourself in the chest trying to keep up.

They kiss once then twice. In betweens kisses the laughs dissolve into a more of a passionate display. Emotions run hot and really heavy. The intentions here are no longer going out to eat but maybe breakfast in the shower and dessert

Mai: Hmm. What you say we go back to my house and um, get out of these sweaty clothes and have breakfast in bed?

As much as he wants to, Chris knows that he can't. He has been here before but not with someone like Maya. The normal pull away won't work without a reason. With an abrupt pause Chris pulls away. Maya feeling her advance being rejected tries to recover.

Mai: What's wrong?

Chris: I don't think that's a good idea right now.

For the first time sex has come up to the forfront of the relationship. You would be amazed that after all this time of dates and hanging out with each other it would have come up before, but it hasn't. Chris had made every attempt to keep things exciting. So dates, outings and creative moments have been more of a way to keep the opportunity for sex at bay. What he didn't realize is that all the stuff that was done may be his saving grace. But at the expense of wowing and woowing women this has done nothing but made him more attractive. Maya is no different than the others. Feeling even more dejected and stupid, quickly this went from hot and heavy to upset. Maya changes her tone. Not too angry but you can tell she is bothered and of course she will deny it.

Mai: You know I just remembered I have to take care of some business for work before Monday. I'm going to go. Come Keno.

Chris: What? What about breakfast?

Mai: I'm not really hungry right now. Do you need me to give you a ride home?

Chris: Nah, I can walk. So … we …can't talk about this?

Mai: There is nothing to talk about.

Chris: Talk to you later?

Mai: Sure.

Watching Maya walk off, Chris feels as if there is nothing he can do. More heartbroken than upset he wonders what does this mean for the future. Maya walking away feels rejected and heartbroken. Her concern is not the future but what does this mean right now. Was it too soon? Should she have let him make the move? Chris and Maya feel the relationship may be in danger and time is the vicious slow turning vice around their hearts. Chris so engaged on what to do now, very easily thoughts of Mysary creep like innocence into his mind. A place he has often turned to when relationships run a rye. Things are different now.

Two people who really never went a moment without at bare minimum text are now beginning to drift. Only in the physical though, something inside both of them is calling the others name reminding Christopher that the harder he tries to let go the more he cares. Mysary as much as she wants to be the Ms. Independent with her feelings she can not deny how he has been her Superman. To make things equally difficult Love throws a curve ball. Mysary has begun to realize how awesome a man Derik truly is and how she has hurt him with her cloaked feelings for Christopher. Christopher has somehow found a woman who is everything Mysary is and she meaning Maya is not taken. Where do things stand now though after a pivotal crossroad has them wondering trying to figure out where do they go from here. Do they continue to walk a way?

At the downtown Track and Fitness Club, Miz exercises her membership to the fullest. Walking barefoot across the stone flooring she positions her suit to the direct level of comfort. Everything around her, even the heat sound of the pool becomes a soft harmony of whispers that fades into the stilled calm of nothingness. The water moans with the echo of hands clapping a massage against its skin. The opposing wave with each stroke and bob exhales in submission and yields to the strength of this satin stone like missile. Like the flow of a sweet amber mist through Egyptian lace she turns around underwater heading back to the point of origin. Her intensity increases, thrusting off the wall and piercing through from eighteen inches deep. Focused, driven, and possessed with the passion for completion, her moves become second nature void of any mental exertion. No longer in competition with time or self, her motions continue as thoughts unrevealed to anyone are now sorted and processed. After several laps in the pool her mind is a sauna of clear thinking. Walking back to the showers she checks her phone to see if there are any messages.

Mysary: Hey, you called?

Derik: Yeah, you at the pool?

Mysary: You know me like a book right? (*subtle hints of sarcasm*)

Derik: How long have we been together now? So everything's cool? (*Still trying to fish for the overall emotion or tone of the air*)

Mysary: I'm chill. So what up?

Derik: I got four tickets to the grand opening of that new dinner theatre in Essex tomorrow night. The featured play is It Could Have Been Me.

Mysary: That's cool. So who are the other tickets for?

Derik: I was thinking you might want to ask Airicka.

Mysary: She went back home for the weekend.

Derik: Well what about Christopher, you did say he was seeing someone now right?

Mysary: I'll ask him when I get home.

Derik: Hey babe, look I know I haven't always been the best when it comes to you and Chris. And I'm not sayin' I'm cool with it now I still have my issues. Not with you or him I guess it's me. I told you before I was never good with this relationship thing and I have done my share of dirt in the past. I feel like I don't deserve a person like you. And because the two of you share something I can't. I feel like he has a part of you that I never will have. (*before the emotions get caught up*) Hey I know you gotta go, we'll talk later.

Mysary: Derik, I Love You.

These moments are what really make, break, or define relationships when the other person buys into what you have been selling all along. And you hear that they are as committed as you. Mysary understands to some extent how Derik has been feeling. Also she recognizes how her denial of what she really feels for Christopher has not been a secret, it has only made life harder for Derik. This would explain why he has been going over board with gifts, dinner these past few weeks. Derik

186

has been fighting against a stacked deck and never once gave up.
Never called it quits when he had every right to. It was her anger over
the Mai situation that finally brought this to light. The love right in
front of her was more than what she had initially seen. After 4 years,
Derik took on the daunting task of giving his all to someone who only
wanted him as a consolation. Say what you want about this but there
are many women who have a great runner up and just don't know it.
Mysary is glad that under the circumstance she can try again. Try to
mend the fence that she has been slowly chipping away. Mysary has
come to the conclusion with obvious reservations still that Christopher
has finally found someone that he wants more than her. Rather than
focus on whether or not she has lost him for good she refuses to be hurt
by rejection and she throws herself into the role of contestant number
two. He is so happy to finally feel his love reciprocated he doesn't care
that she is rebounding from a luv she never actually had.

Sometime later the next day in Derik's loft, Mysary and Derik are
sitting at the table eating ice cream making jokes like they normally do.
It's these playful moments when if you're not careful can turn into
more than playtime.

Derik: (*As he feeds Miz*) You know, I thought this would be hard at
first.

Mysary: What? (*As the soft taste of dark indulgence glides to places*
that invoke thoughts of serenity)

Derik: The no sex thing? It's not all that hard anymore.

187

[Mysary] What the hell does he mean it ain't that hard? Oh what are you trying to say. We'll see how much trouble it's not.

Taking to heart the words he said, Mysary waits for the next chocolate to be fed. The only way the next set of events can be described is like this: Amaretto and butterscotch crème whispers breathe like kisses for the soul as fingers are relaxed on lips leaving a trail of coco tears. Time is utterly motionless as thoughts and actions collide, a harmony of rainbow scented fabrics of what our bodies desperately craved to be clothed in. Eyes explode like the Indonesian pimple of 1883 all of our pleasures unveiled to the tune when it feels like one of those nights that wall screams as they fall to pieces from the tension. Looking so deep inside, you trade places just to experience the joyous sensation of being one with the night. Seconds seem to lay hold to the delusion that they are eons as you feel like this moment is all that matters there are no consequences. Lips lock, as the dance of the bodies begins. Spinning is the room quiet, thoughts careen out of control as clothes escape your pours as if they are allergic. Less than two feet away from the Sealy's edge the moment is stopped.

Derik: Wait. (*Between kisses*) Wait um. We can't do this bae. As much as I want to, Ooo! And I really want to.

Miz: Well what's stopping you?

Intensifying her efforts running fingers around his neck. He struggles with holding her, letting go often giving into the desire to free her from space to the luxury of his arms. Intoxicated by the still present aroma of coconut and honey she pushes away knowing she wants to resist but continues. Savoring every last ounce of this closeness their bodies begin to breathe almost like they're one. Reluctantly forcing the break Derik gets up and goes into the kitchen. Miz feeling a little rejected, tears of frustration are overshadowed by the ability to compensate for a temporary loss of self-control. The true weight of what just went on will never really be understood.

Miz: I know. Thank you.

Derik: For what?

Miz: Just being you. Now get the hell out of my way, the Mercedes twins need a cold shower.

As if one long chill goes up and down his spin, his eyes stop as a soft deviant smile relieves his face from blank stare.

Miz: What was that all about?

Derik: The visual.

Miz: Well you want to come join me?

Derik: Riiiiiight. Just go.

Miz: You sure?

Dropping the rest of clothes to the floor Derik quickly turns away looking down trying effortlessly not to look at the mirror.

Derik: Quit playing. I'm in the kitchen you want anything?

Miz: Don't ask me that right now. You know what I want.

Derik: Would like something to eat?

Miz mouthing the words from behind clinched teeth you know how bad I want you right now. It's too hard to breathe goes beyond the boundaries of silence to grab the attention of Derik .

Derik: What was that?

Miz: Huh? Nothing.

Escaping quickly to the other side of the loft. Turning on the shower trying to maintain a conversation over the sound of steaming hot massage powered tear drops. Of course it never works. Before entering the kitchen Derik cranks up the tunes. The open space allows the sound to dance through the air clearing the tension of the moment. Getting ready for tonight, Mysary thinks as the shower attempts to relax her hormones. There is always that part of you that wants to give in so bad to the madness no matter how small overwhelms the calm. This is one of those times when the strength of their conviction and promise to God is made to prevail.

[MYSARY] This is why I luv this man and at the same time I want this man. Four years of putting up with all my ways. Honoring my commitment and the way he has been supporting me is wonderful.

This is one of those times when I really want to say to hell with it all and just do it. I guess I'm alone in that huh?

It's about 6:35 p.m., en route to pick up Maya for what could be a very interesting night. For the first time since high school, a double date. You would think that having been friends for so many years that at least they would have tried it once or twice. Some of you might say that is just tempting fate with all those emotions and insecurities, some real stuff could jump off. Miz and Chris haven't really dealt with the effects of the incident at Shelia's. They have by circumstance not really crossed paths, creating a tidal wave of questions and emotions. So with the text and invite to dinner Chris figured things were resolved or this was an attempt to apologize and move on.

At a table in the back of Tony's, Miz and Derik can see the front door and the stage. Sipping on San Pellegrino the conversation is not focused on the events of earlier more about the future.

Derik: So have you given any more thought to what you're going to do?

Mysary: Some. I mean, if I stay I have to find a place. Don't try to say I can stay with you after today that might not be a good idea.

Derik: You right. I won't bring it up. Is there anything I can do to sway your decision?

Mysary: No. You've made your case quite clear.

Derik: Ok, so what can you tell me about Chris' new girl? You have met her right?

Certainly not to reveal the crisis of conflict as if she knew how to verbalize it anyway Miz responds with the casual answer.

Mysary: She's cute, she's got a face.

Derik: I would hope so. Faces I think are a standard out of the womb accessory.

Mysary: What, if you would let me finish, I would have told you she has a face like your cousin Monique maybe a few shades darker. She is about my height.

Derik: Well, I'm glad he got somebody. So you think this one will last?

Knowing damn well he's hoping this one will last to ease the pressure off of him to compete.

Mysary: We haven't seen too much of each other so I couldn't say, but he seems happy.

At that moment the next wave of guests come into the Main area of the restaurant. In the confusion Derik, can see Christopher being lead to the table by the hostess, but he is unable to see his date. Nudging Miz he points to where Chris is, as he approaches the table. Miz the constant queen of controlling a situation tries to eye Mai quickly to

192

prepare for round two of the face to face.

You know you have those moments where the strangest things happen. Chris moves to the left and after pulling out her chair Mai avails from behind Chris looking to her right with a soft but serious smile greeting Miz and moving one more over their eyes explode in a Oh my God I can't believe it's you. Miz catches a glimps of something but they quickly break the tie and now the internal quarrels begin. Miz and Chris are playing it so cool they don't realize the tension between Maya and Derik. So now there is this really ackward four-way tension going on.

Chris: Hey, sorry we're late. You know how traffic can be this time of night. Mai Luv This is Derik and you know Mysary.

Derik: Mai is it, that's and interesting name is short for...

Chris quick to intervene asserting his prowess as the man.

Chris: Maya, It's short for Maya.

As Mai takes her seat, Chris pushing it in before he takes his own. Maya and Derik smile that uncomfortable smile that really says, "What are you doing here?" Chris and Miz both wonder whats going on with the other. Mysary still doesn't understand what the song meant nor why Chris never mentioned this new girl. Christopher is sitting between Luv and Mysary. There is no ability to have real fun the focus is more on keeping the facade of the how in the hell did this happen. Holding on to secret accounts rather than reconcile is the spice that fires the

193

*gumbo of self inflicted tourment. We often define happiness by the
amount of personal conflict we can develop. So then i ask if it is easier
to be honest with one another and to speak from the heart then why
don't we?*

*The night was pleasant. Christopher and Mysary pretending all is well
when it clearly isn't. Derik and Maya avoiding looking too obvious, try
to hide their secret. Luckily the dinner theatre had very dim lighting or
everyone would be on blast. With it being a show there was a reason
not to talk much. You know how it is when couples go out they usually
hang out after the show and talk the night away, especially when no
one is having sex. These four waste no time in leaving after the show.*

Chris: Hey D, thanks again for the invite. Miz, see you later?

Derik: No prob, glad you could make it and Maya, nice to meet you.

*This was no ordinary drive home Derik's heart is pounding, Mysary
covering up any emotions. To hide any problem they try to make chit
chat but then comes that moment of unexpected silence and out of
which the question blindsides you.*

Mysary: So what was that back there?

Derik: What was what back where?

Mysary: That Look

Derik quickly playing back memories trying to pin point the reference

194

of what she could be talking about. When he really knows what she is talking about but he can't tell her.

Derik: Okay, I'm lost, what look?

While driving he can't tell if she saw the small change in his body language. He must continue as if she didn't see a thing.

Mysary: That look between you and Maya?

Derik: Nothing

Mysary: That didn't look like a nothing look to me.

Derik: What did it look like then?

You must be certain not to pose the question with the sound being defensive or having something to hide. Spending so much time and energy on fostering a response you can easily forget the person where your comments will be directed is also thinking as well.

Mysary: What a cop out?

Derik: What?

Mysary: You heard me what a cop out. That misdirection is so third grade. I ask you because I wanted to know which meant I know that there was some meaning hence the reason for my question.

Derik never let's go of the secret and with a candid sense of calm he
tries to let the moment pass. If there is one thing you come to realize in
a long term relationship, is that an unspoken look means now dead air
has become more of an instigator than an ally.

[Derik] I'm not even sure what that look meant, its been how long
now? Until I know for sure what it meant I'm not saying jack.

Derik: It was nothing ai'ght.

Mysary: Humph.

Most would walk head on into this mine field but after four years Derik
knows he can avoid all confrontation by just letting it go for now or
delivering the common "You're Right". He realizes though this is not
the end of this conversation he only needs to be ready.

The rain poured like inconsistent kisses from that of an unrequited love.
Derik waits inside a small coffee house after a phone call to Maya. Is
this wrong to meet with an ex and not tell? Is there something to tell?
He doesn't know what drove him to meet her here of all places. He
really had nothing to hide. But still seeing her the other night brought
back some feelings Derik thought had died. Why did she have to be
with him of all people? He wonders has she told him about their past;
damn that has got to make for some interesting conversations. With
each passing second Derik tries think of what he is going to say.
Maybe she won't show and he can be mad enough to forget these
emotions. Who the hell is he kidding?

196

The mental conversation broke as if he knew that moment would be the moment she would walk in. The breeze and rain followed her as she removed her jacket and relaxed her umbrella. Maya is greeted by one of her friends slash former coworkers, who is now in the role of manager, a position she trained him for.

Maya: Hey Marv how's it going?

Marvin: Good haven't seen you around in a while. Nice to see you again. I believe the gentleman you are looking for is in the back at table 12.

Maya: Hey Marvin can i get...

Before she could finish the statement Marvin intercepts.

Marvin: ... Low fat Mocha Smoothie with skim milk no whip cream but extra butternut fudge, right? You taught me well.

Maya: That I did. Can you bring it to the table, please?

Marvin: Be glad too.

Their eyes connect with semi formal greeting. The wounds of the past wrapped in the scent of "Damn you look good" seem to catch the breeze for a faint moment. Then it is the questions surrounding, why here? Why now? Drawing closer Derik stands. The track on the ambiance changes to Don't Take My Girl Away

Derik: Hey. Wow you look amazing.

Maya: I do don't I? What's up?

Doing the semi twirl thing to show of how the past few years without him have done me so well. Some would consider this to be an arrogant move on my part, but let me ask you something? Would you allow anyone to know how deep they hurt you if it took you this long to get over them? So then you understand I have to let him know I am doing just find. Am I right? Thought you would see it my way.

Maya: This better be important if I'm going to come out in the rain. So, what's up?

Derik: Nothing much. How have you been?

Maya: Fine Derik. (*Not in a pissed off way. More like after exhaling and with a soft smile.*)Okay enough with the formalities, why did you call?

Derik: Yo, I don't know. I mean I saw you the other night it brought back some serious memories. I didn't know what to think, what to say.

Maya: What you still doing with my number, I know your new chick ain't feeling that.

Derik: Look it's been almost 4 years since we even saw each other. Let alone spoke. So to see you there with him was heavy.

Maya: What does that mean? What does who I'm seeing have to do with the price of tea in China?

Derik: Nothing, can I ask you something?

Maya: You just did.

Derik: For real man.

Maya: Okay, you need to stop leaving yourself so open.

Forgoing the obvious diss for a more major thought that consumes his mind. You would think he was trying to pop the question the way he is reacting. Hands start to sweat as the thought of breathing escapes him for the moment after a long deep sigh.

Derik: Look you know I'm no good at this. Trying to express and shit.

Maya: What is this? Just say it.

Derik: Yo, it ain't that easy. I feel like I need to apologize for the way things went down. If it means anything to you.

Maya: Look Derik, thank you for wanting to see me and all. I hope you got the closure you needed.

Derik: In a way I did but I really have to thank you.

Maya: What for? I mean there have been so many things.

With that classic smile, for a brief moment hearts go back to a gentler time when they were one. As quick as they landed in that memory; they return even quicker to the realm of the here and now. But the baggage of those heaven sweet instances wasn't left behind. Slowly those fragrant smiles are subtly replaced with a nodding deep sigh.

Derik: Nah on the real. Thank you for helping me to become who I am.

Maya: And what did I help to create?

Derik: Quit playing man. You know what I mean. You put up with a lot and after you left...

Maya: You broke it off with me remember. And I wasn't playing I would like to know what type of product has my name attached to it. Never mind it's in the past anyway don't sweat it.

Derik: True but...

Not really sure of her meaning or her thought process he just tries to continue his initial statement. His thoughts just ramble between what his feelings are about her and why does it bother him that his personal nemesis now has two of his women. I guess you could say this is that territorial thing about men.

[Derik] Okay, you reading this tell me is it wrong that I feel like this dude owns territory in my present and is now buying property in my past? Shit.

Derik: Look I really learned how to listen more talk less. More important I figured out I don't have to fix everything.

Maya: So let me ask what was with the whole abrupt leaving thing.

Derik: I just had to um. I mean I needed to. I don't have a good reason I was stupid.

Mai with a little bit of candid sarcasm holds in the thought. "Oh, I'm so glad I could make you better for someone else." With slow fluttering eyes combined and with a thought intense nod she manages to maintain her composure with relaxed arms.
Maya: That's good.

Derik: What?

Maya: You, admitting the truth. We have been down a long road together and that is one thing that hurt me the most. You had no real reason for leaving me and after I had finally given you all of me and what seem like security was snatched away from me and what did that leave me with?

Derik: I hurt you I know but that is not what this is about.

Maya: Then what really, I mean after four years you see me with someone else and you just out of the blue want to rehash old times? Thanks, but no thanks.

Derik: Honestly I didn't think it would go down like this.

201

Maya: What was supposed to happen then?

Derik: Back then I wasn't sure what was going on. My parents were breaking up after what seem to be a perfect marriage.

Maya: Derik, the marriage wasn't perfect. They just shielded you from the turmoil.

Derik: I saw us as a newer version of them. Then as things started to dwindle I realized they were just surviving each other for the sake of the image. You had to know I luv'd you and I didn't want us to end up like that, I tried to mirror what my dad was doing rather than figure out what was meant for me to know. I wasn't ready for you.

Maya: I see. So this new chick is more your speed?

Derik: She's a lot like you? [Why in the Hell did I say that?]

Maya: So I was some sort of trial run. I work out all the lumps and someone else gets the reward.

Derik: Nah, you know you were my heart

Maya: And that makes me better how exactly?

Derik: Look I didn't ask you here to argue. As I said before I am not sure what we are doing here. I just knew I had to see you. I had to talk to you. You wanted to see me too, right? Why else would you be here?

When you meet with an ex sometimes you say and feel things that seem to open a door to the past or you're exposed to the other person in a new light. Then, I want you back for some odd reason light. Or you look so much better to me now then I am with someone else light. When all that has happened is the weight of you is no longer their burden and they look free. The normalcy of your current relationship good or bad doesn't look as sweet as what you can't have. So does desire set in and if so do you act on it? Then what?

Derik and Maya continue to talk. The time has eased the tension and changed the mode. The longer they stay though the more dangerous it could become. Thoughts can quickly become actions, especially when they know the other all too well. Both get messages and phone calls from their respective others, but as the conversation gets comfortable they seem to forget obligations. The music of the coffee shop jumps right in on playing the soundtrack to their past. It begins to water dormant feelings. There is a look they share that can't be easily explained. It's the Frankenstein of I miss you stitched in some mad scientist pattern to I wish I never came. Regret before anything happens awakens the monster. Maya looks at her watch realizing how late it is, thinks it's best they go their own way and never speak of this. Then they hug on accident like tradition and for a moment they look as if they would kiss.

Maya: You don't want to do this

Derik: Do what?

Maya: This, whatever you're thinking. Don't.

Unbeknownst to them Janet and Neecie have walked into the coffee shop and are at the counter ordering two Civet Coffees. Janet not 100% sure asks Neecie if that is Mysary's Derik on another woman. Of course technology being what it is, the image is captured and sent via text to Mysary with the text "I thought this was something you might need to see". Derik and Maya break the embrace, Maya goes to the restroom Derik sits at the table with his hands folded. Thoughts of what have I done? What did I start? run ramped in their minds. They leave to go their separate ways but they are tied together by memories.

About 4:30 the next day Mysary and Raven are finishing up talks about the wedding. Mysary on her way to meet Derik at Cafe Intermezzo is still dealing with so many thoughts. The cost of being all woman is that there is no one to count on when you're the anchor. Thinking about what does it mean when the man who you have held out on for so long visits an ex. Personal examination leads to questions of inadequacies locked behind the walls of true perception a moment of weakness leaks out. Only during alone times do these moments hurt so much yet you can never share these moments with friends because they couldn't handle to see you like that. And the one person you could honestly go to; you let pride hinder the call for help, so now you build up the strength to break on through to the other side. Gathering your thoughts is not as easy this time...

Derik: Hey sweetie glad you could make it.

Miz: Yeah I said I would be here.

Derik: You'll never guess what happened today. Angie tells Donte

Both realizing something is not right but the moment is overshadowed by his dominance to make it okay and her reluctance to depend on anyone but herself. Who will be the first to budge?

Derik: Hey Luv, I was thinking we could go out of town next weekend. I found this little get away spot.

Mysary: Derik, we need to talk.

Derik: Ok, what's up?

Mysary: The other night when we were out at the theatre. Chris' friend Maya...

RUN FOOL! This can't be good. It's a set up bruh and you ain't ready. Sorry bout writing, this I got a little close to the situation.

Derik: Ah, yeah what about it?

Mysary: You never finished telling me what did that look mean.

Derik: Oh, um. We ah, had seen each other before somewhere

Mysary: Hm. That didn't look like oh hey you.

Derik: Well what did it look like?

Mysary: That's what I want to know, is there something you want to tell me?

At this moment you can tell the truth. The person on the other end knows something so lying is not in your best interest. However, if you don't know what you are confessing to then you do what is inherent deny everything. Let's see how that works.

Derik: What are you saying? (*He can tell she is fishing for something*)

Mysary: (*She will not show the picture. After 3 yrs why should she? Derik is not like the other guys he has no reason to lie or hide anything?*) Look we are out in public and this will not be one of those crazy psycho girlfriend moments. Here it is, I know that there was more to it than just a look so, are you going to tell me or what?

Derik: Look, there was nothing to it? We saw each other recognized each other then that was it.

Mysary: You sure?

Derik: That's all it was.

Mysary: Ok then.

You never want to assume the worst but often we find it hard to believe the best in people. This is still an unresolved issue but now the issue of trust is broken, the longer it goes unattended the harder it will be to repair.

Mysary: What do you have planned for next weekend?

Derik: Nothing much really going to hang with a friend in the morning, then I am free. Why, what's up?

Mysary: Nothing. Was there something you wanted to talk to me about?

Derik: Yeah, but I forgot what it was.

Mysary: Well I have to go.

Derik responds with an "Ok, text me later". As they leave Derik tries get one of those new kisses, but it's as if Mysary has reverted back to the way things used to be. Derik, a little thrown doesn't put two and two together; he figures she may just be tired. Like a great agent Mysary covers her emotions well. Once she is in the car the questions and thoughts are dissected and placed carefully in row. Of all people why her? Who is she to Derik? Why would he have to lie about it? Coming home angry and upset is never a good combination. What tends to make it worse is when you conceal the pain from those closest to you. Even in the midst of being at odds with your best friend, you know they are always willing to set aside their own differences to ensure that nothing serious has happened. Christopher is not at home but Miz could really use that friend who for years has put up with her craziness.

This time it's a state of emergency. She has to tell him about the photo. That right there though could be a whole different can of worms. This could be the opening she needs to mend their relationship.

It's become more than a ritual, Christopher and Mai ending the day together. They have become like a make shift family. She meets him at Cold Spring then before picking up her sister at the after school program they hit the park with Keno for a nice stroll weather permitting or they just pick up her sister and they return to Mai's place. Ever since the first time they kissed Mai often wondered why Chris never tried to take things to another level, a more physical one but for fear of sounding fast or even worse ruining a good thing she never asked. Now with the Derik thing in the picture she wonders if it will get anymore crazy. The thoughts of whether or not Chris is into Mysary have all but vanished but as a woman in the back of her mind she doesn't forget the look she got that night at the club and what it seem to insinuate. Like any other relationships there have been disagreements they usually end with a few days of silence or the immediate make up a few hours later over the phone. This night was a little different in that Chris was interested in deep conversation. How is this different from any other time you ask? Well it starts with the sun setting behind the condos across the street. Looking out the window Chris suggest they sit outside and talk. Leaving the front door cracked, bringing a pillow, the cordless phone, and a glass of half and half outside they enjoy the sights and the sounds of the city.

Chris: Let me ask you something, do you think men and women can just be friends. Nah wait scratch that.

Mai: Okay, Harry…

Chris: I was hoping you wouldn't catch that. What I meant to say was do you think that relationships are based on wants & needs from both?

Mai: What do you mean?

Chris: Well, remember a while ago when we were on the subject of relationships? I brought it up to Sam and Tischa.

Mai: Really? What did they say? Or should I ask what you said?

Chris: I just said what I said to you about the condition by which a relationship grows is strictly based on what is wanted and if the current placeholder can fill that need.

Mai: I see, so what about us?

Realizing the touchy waters he has begun to tread, Chris tries like all men to maneuver carefully through this conversation not sure the type of mine field he has landed in.

Chris: With all due respect I see no difference in us. This is not a bad thing or a good thing. It is what it is.

Mai: Oh please explain.

Chris: Sure, whatever it was that brought us together that day in the park was the catalyst. Our lives were on a path that would meet at that moment. Our conversation started from an initial attraction, the want and need to continue was a product of mutual interest.

Mai: The jury is still out. Please continue, you know I like listening to you talk.

Chris: Well jump in anytime. Where was I?

Mai: You were talking about mutual interest.

Chris: Oh yeah, wouldn't you agree?

Mai: Agree to what?

Chris: That we both wanted that conversation?

Mai: True, but where does the need come in?

Chris: That's simple. At that exact moment we needed whatever the experience was to be real. I am sure that you have had your fair share of dude's that look good on paper but never pan out. I have seen enough females to know that sometimes there is beautiful wrapping but a few things missing on the inside.

Mai: I see.

At that moment Christopher's phone rings. Normally he would check the number and reject the call but it's Mysary. Something is telling him to answer. Even to the clear disapproval of Maya. She doesn't see who's calling, just the fact that their conversation was interrupted. Not wanting to appear too upset she waits.

Chris: Hey. (*With a calm kind of indifference*) What up?

Miz: Are you busy?

Chris: No why?

Miz: I need you.

The words you long to hear at a time when you shouldn't want to hear them.

Miz: How soon can you get hear?

No pondering do you ask for her car to help a friend? What if she has 20 questions? Chris has never given any thought to tell Maya who is on the other end.

Chris: In about 15 – 20 minutes.

Miz: Thanks. See you in a bit.

Chris: No problem.

PROBLEM. You see it coming don't you; well let's not waist time.

Chris: Hey bae, a friend of mine needs my help with something. Is it ok if I borrow your car to help them out?

Mai: Ah, weren't we in the middle of something? Is it an emergency?

Chris: Yes, we were and normally I wouldn't have answered the phone but something was telling me it was important. It didn't sound like a dire emergency but it did sound rather important. If it's a problem I could call Sam to come get me.

Maya is stewing over how to respond. She is upset but doesn't want to start asking more questions because it is apparent that he is going to leave anyway. Nothing that she can say right now will make him stay. Allowing trust to take hold she hands him the keys. They kiss for a second and just like that he's gone. No reason and no explanation just a kiss and no I love you. Maya left to ponder and stew over how she feels. The more she thinks the more she gets hot about the situation. Imagine if she new it was Mysary on the other end. I'm afraid to ask how you would respond. Although Maya gives the ok this will be waiting when he gets back.

Getting home Mysary is in the kitchen when Christopher comes in the door. This is really the first friend-to-friend moment they have had in a long time.

Chris: Hey man, what's up?

Mysary is almost amazed that he came and at the same time is so thankful that he did. Her eyes brighten and a smile of "Oh how I really need you." over takes her face as he answers the call to swoop in and save the day.

Miz: Hey, you weren't busy were you?

Chris: You sounded like you needed my help with something. I wasn't busy but I was doing something.

Miz: So, we haven't really had the opportunity to talk

Chris: Ok, what is really going on?

Miz: What do you mean?

Chis: I've known you how long right? So when I see you and you start in on the cover questions I know something is up, or seriously wrong. Well.?

Miz: Well what?

Chris a little bothered by the cat and mouse. Mysary sensing it not wanting to argue blurts out...

Miz: I think, the fact that Derik and I haven't done it; he may be finally tired of waiting and getting it from somewhere else.

Christopher going from bothered to what did you say in a short span of time is torn between "How could he?" and asking "Why you wait til now to do this?"

Chris: That's a petty strong accusation. What makes you think something like that?

Torn between the thought of showing or not showing the picture on her phone is the dilemma, for fear it could be less than what it is. So with out concrete evidence she chooses not to.

Miz: Neecie thought she saw him hugged up with some woman. And not hugged up in a "hey how you doing" kind of way.

Chris: Word? So did you ask him about it?

Miz: Yeah but that's just it. How do you ask that question? You don't just say, (*altering her voice to sound like a laughable version of a psycho girlfriend*) "Are you cheatin' on me?"

Chris: To tell the truth, yes. Don't play games the two of you have been together for a minute (*As much as it pains him, he never ask do you luv him*) so just come right out with it. He's either going to say yes or no; its up to you to believe him or not.

Miz: You're right. I shouldn't assume anything. (*Wanting so desperately to show the picture in her phone she doesn't. At this moment she wants to ask a million and one questions but she doesn't. All she does is...*) Thank you for coming Chris. I hope I didn't cause any trouble.

Chris wanting to say so many things to Mysary now, but he doesn't. So desperately wanting to show her how he really feels even with another love waiting for him but he doesn't. All he does is.

Chris: Anytime you know that.

Then there was this awkward pause and silence.

Chris: Well I should go

214

Mysary: Ok, then

Sending him off to be with her. A part off him caught up in the here and now wants to hear stay with me. It never happens so Chris leaves and the closing of the door is more symbolic of their status as old friends. On the ride back to Maya's Chris begins to feel guilty as if something wrong was done. Who is the feeling of guilt for though?

Chris: Hey bae, I'm back.

Mai: We need to talk.

Chris: Ok. (*Leaning in for a kiss Maya shuns the advanceand counters with*) Hmph. What is up? (*With a hint of caution.*)

Mai: I don't appreciate you leaving.

Chris: What? Are you serious?

Mai: Damn straight.

Chris: Whoa, now fall back with that.

Mai: Fall back with what?

Chris: Look, if you going to be mad be mad. For the life of me I don't know why. But you don't have to cuss at me.

Mai: Are You Serious?

215

Chris: Ya damn straight. Why are you trippin anyway, I asked you if it was ok and you said yeah.

Mai: What point would it have made to say no? You already made up your mind to leave.

Chris: Look, I don't get this, I asked you if it was okay and you said it was chill.

Mai: You seem to be missing the point here.

Chris: And that is?

Mai: We were into a conversation that I felt was getting deep. Then out of nowhere you get a call and you are gone.

Chris: Maybe I am missing something here. You said you were cool.

Mai: Would you quit saying that!

Chris: Then please help me understand what is going on? If it was... I mean you said what you said then all of sudden it is null and void.

Mai: Forget it!

Chris: Nah, you did that before and I ain't about to go through that again.

Mai: What?

Chris: That forget it mess. That's for the birds.

Mai: And what does that mean?

Chris: We're going to hash this mess out.

Mai: Or?

Chris: It's not going to be no or.

Mai: So you understand how I feel.

Chris: No.

Mai: It's the same thing.

Chris: This is in no way the same things as that. It's crazy to compare the two.

Mai: Oh so I'm crazy now?

Chris: Are you listening to what you're saying?

Mai: Yes I'm hearing quite clearly.

Chris: You must not be. I never said you were crazy.

217

Mai: Look, it doesn't matter you shouldn't have left. That's all I'm sayin'.

Chris: I'm not about to apologize for anything. I still don't get it why you mad.

Mai: Oh so this friend couldn't call someone else you were the only one in this entire city that could help them right?

Chris: Look, if you are going to be this petty about it. I'ma bounce

Mai: Do what you gotta?

Chris: Really? It's like that?

Mai: Like what, Chris? Either you're going to go or you're not. Your mind is already made up anyway. What does it matter what I say?

Chris: Do you have something to say?

Mai: Would it make a difference?

Chris: I'm still here aren't I?

Mai: Yeah, I guess.

The tension has subsided but the memory is hot and fresh. There is a silence that goes on for feels like an hour. The call and response is Chris asking, "So what now?" to Maya's reply, "I don't know" scatter

through out the extended quiet. Now there have been minor arguments, disagreements that were resolved in longer time a few days, a week even. This right here an argument that never really gets resolved maybe a sign of something bigger brewing. It is about that time when the novelty or newness wears off. I guess we'll have to keep an eye on things between these two.

Airicka has been trying to make a case for Brevin at the same time trying to determine if Renee is the better choice. It's very unnerving all those times they profess to luv her, but making her choose between the two is not luv is it? The stress has become so heavy a burden that while at home alone her mind has managed to foster images of both Brevin and Renee. Then to top it off as she writes down her thoughts the two of them try to carry on a conversation. Both voices overlap creating a tango of confusion between imagination and reality

[Airicka]Trying hard to control my heart. I need only the feel of you to fill me up. Take this body and use it as you please with minds alike you know the touch of ease. The weight of your stare is hypnotic my hands loose all control of their natural function and I...

Renee: Are you okay?

Airicka: How can I respond, my thoughts are absent at this moment you are just... I can't begin to think about you. My mind and heart wish not to know who you are just continue to embrace me whole, let not the words of experience impede the process of release can't you see how much I need this to be right. No time for silly thoughts of here we go again and the tales of remorse to follow. I only want the feeling inside that makes all other thoughts go away.

Brevin: You seem a little more tense than usual. Would you like a massage?

[Airicka] Well if you must. For whatever reason you think this is pleasing. The gentle parade of tips injecting comfort into every pore as

220

our colors blend to a whispered gradient of soft cries and obscure rainbows. I'm not moving in with you. There I said it, are you happy?

Renee & Brevin: It just isn't fair

Renee: The nights you like to lay wet with my kiss

Brevin & Renee: and I can't take my place with you because...

Renee: You don't have to say anything I can feel the day all over you.

Airicka: Right you feel me. Then why can't I say no to you? How come I never resist you? Everytime we are here its like seven thousand six hundred and sixty-nine individually wrapped moments of clamorous behavior. How does that feel? Please tell me so I can with an inkling of comprehension label this.

Brevin: I'll be right back. You need anything?

Airicka: How can you just up and let me go like that. I ache for the silent confession of you. Maybe it's wrong, maybe it's unfair to want you to melt into my veins over and over to the point of utter numbness.

Renee: See that didn't take long; are you any better?

Airicka: Better right. Why are you here? What do you want from me?

Brevin & Renee: Be honest with me. You said you want me.

Airicka: And just like that you are gone. Like a pro of the snatch & stab the only thing left are the quiet tears I bleed. I don't know how I got to this place in my life I look at everything and I just don't know.

Brevin: Well you could always **Renee:** Move in with me

Brevin & Renee: I promise no strings

Airicka: You don't want me. I am just fulfilling some desire you have. That sucks. Can you say you love me and mean it? ...Thought not.

The struggle in her mind of past voices beats down on her with a vengance. Not making her choices any easier. Renee wants her to move in so she can officially change her status. Secretly Brevin feels if he moves her in with him, her lifestyle and his randomness will change. The question for both of them is how can you change what you didn't create? So hung up on themselves that they don't realize what it's doing to Airicka. To top it all off she remembers the last thing her father said and the weight it brings.

Airicka's Father: (*voice echoing in her head*) When your daughter looks at you that first time and says she wants a man like her daddy. There are so many ways to share that joy and none of them really express it right. As a direct counter when she looks at you and says I hope I never find a man like you. Death wrapped in a thunderstorm of hell may scratch the surface. And when she gets older you hope she looks back and before your last breath just call you daddy again. I'm sorry baby girl...

Airicka: Why did you leave me? I could never forgive… Oh GOD! Why does this hurt so much I want to hate him. Why can't I get them out of my mind? What did I do? WHY WON'T ANY BODY LOVE ME? I'm tired of hurting I just want to be held is that too much to ask…

The darkness is broken by the sounds of crushed whimpers released for the first time. Yes, beautiful people cry too. It's amazing how you grow up in a single parent home and everybody idolizes you about how pretty you are and how good your hair is. My personal favorite is you gonna be a heartbreaker when you get older. Never mind the fact men two to three times your age were always leering at you in secret. Some close friends of the family who wanted the title of uncle just to cop a quick feel from a hug or use the memory of that soft butternut complexion to slowly guide their hand up and down the shaft to gism land. Though never physically being molested the mental anguish of being raped by eyes and words haunt you in that lonely room. Girls always accused you of breaking them up from their boyfriends wanting to fight you over their insecurities. No one wanted to be your friend they always think you were conceited or a snobb because you're quiet and you also had a brain. From behind the cover of fainted juniper candles and the melody of "[18]Sorrow & Misery" there is a gentle knock at the door. Never giving thought to answer until the sense of care leads one to open the door slow. A strong and caressing voice breezes through the crack.

Airicka: Why did you leave me. I could never forgive… Oh GOD!

---

[18] Play track Sorrow and Misery

Why does this hurt so much I want to hate him. Why can't I get them out of my mind. What did I do? WHY WON'T ANY BODY LOVE ME? I'm tired of hurting I just want to be held is that to much to ask...

The darkness is broken by the sounds of crushed whimpers released for the first time. Yes, beautiful people cry too. it's amazing how you grow up in a single parent home and everybody idolizes you about how pretty you are and how good your hair is. My personal favorite is you gonna be a heartbreaker when you get older. Never mind the fact men two to three times your age were always leering at you in secret. Some close friends of the family who wanted the title of uncle just to cop a quick feel from a hug or use the memory of that soft butternut complexion to slowly guide their hand up and down the shaft to gism land. Though never physically being molested the mental anguish of being raped by eyes and words haunt you in that lonely room. Girls always accused you of breaking them up from their boyfriends wanting to fight you over their insecurities. No one wanted to be your friend they always think you were conceited or a snobb because you're quiet and you also had a brain. From behind the cover of fainted juniper candles and the melody of "[19]Sorrow & Misery" there is a gentle knock at the door. Never giving thought to answer until the sense of care leads one to open the door slow. A strong and caressing voice breezes through the crack.

Chris: Ay oh, shorty everything a'ight?

A response is failed by the attempts to pull it together for the usual cast

---

[19] Play track "Nobody Knows You When You're Down And Out"

224

off. Sensing the need, Chris enters the room to assess the situation. Finally reaching the bed where Airicka was nestled in the uttermost corner with his hand he touches her arm. Unspoken words are the best at the beginning they give the person in pain the chance to see where your heart is. The final chords drift right into the melodies of try a little tenderness.

Chris: Airicka?

Airicka: Yeah?

By the sound of her tone no more words were needed at this time. Gently sitting on the bed he begins to comfort her. Ultimately they are friends beyond the point of just hi and bye and the typical difference of opinion. After a few, he gesture for her to sit up and although resistant at first she eventually gives in. Swollen eyes hidden behind tissue-clinched hands are wiped as Airicka shakes her head in brokenness. The coolest thing about Chris is his uncanny ability to lay aside his problems to help a friend. With a strong embrace of security not wanting of anything Airicka breaks down like a soft ice cream cone on a summer day. The tears fall hard and fast as his hands speak calm like the horse whisperers' kiss.

After about a half hour of emptying and comforting some form of utterances are made. Trying to get out all the bottled up issues that had her so bound.

Airicka: I'm sorry I know you got your own problems to be bothered with me.

225

Trying to pull away as she feels like a burden; Chris takes the time to assure her that it is okay to let it out.

Chris: Don't sweat it man. We may not have seen eye to eye on everything but you are good people. Is it something you wanted to talk about?

Airicka: Not right now. I just needed to cry... I think the last time I cried like that was when my father told me about my mother. I'll never forget it was two days after my 10th birthday when he told me the whole story. My father told me that he really loved my mother and they were planning to get married before they found out they were going to have me. He said the day he found out was the same day he proposed. I can remember like it was yesterday, we were sitting in my room and he said, "Baby girl I need to talk to you." He said your old enough now to know the truth. When most girls are getting the birds and bees talk I'm getting this. He said my mother knew she might not survive the delivery and she never told him. She had written this letter and had the doctor give it to him when the time was right. He gave me the letter so I would always have a piece of her with me. I never saw my daddy cry but I could tell that day was as hard for him as it was for me. I felt like when I was younger he held me so close like he didn't want to lose me either. So when he started dating again and that attention was gone I felt like he didn't want me any more because I reminded him too much of her. From that point I never felt like I had a place, a friend to... I mean how could he not love me anymore? What did I do to...

Falling into Chris' shoulder the storm of tears melt against the cold stare of the night. Able to be a friend in this time spoke so much to her road to healing. For the longest he'd said nothing and let his action do all the talking. It is something about the way a man can make even the hardest moments seem like it will be all right. Sensing a space to provide words of emotional encouragement. With the delicate nature of the softest piece of Persian lace and the breeze of a caressing summer night Chris gives a little part of himself.

Chris: Airicka, I say this with all seriousness, I love you.

Airicka: Thanx. I'm glad somebody does.

Chris: Look man, don't let people try to tell you who you are or what you should be doing with your life. You do you and the rest will fall into place.

Airicka: Yeah, but it still hurts the way everybody looks at me with their tawdry innuendos. It's been going on all my life. You'd think I would be past it now.

Chris: Is there anything I can do?

Airicka: I don't even know. I'm moving out. Before you and Miz leave I decided to go now.

Chris: You got a place?

Airicka: Renee needs a new roommate since hers moved out. Brevin offered me the extra room in his condo.

Chris: Ok so you decided?

Airicka: Not sure yet. Told them I would make a decision by Thursday. Most of my stuff is in storage but I need help moving clothes and little things. Can you help?

Chris: You know you got that (*Yawning*).

Airicka: I'm sorry. I didn't mean to keep you up I know you got a lot to do tomorrow I'll be alright.

Chris: Nah man fa real, I was just checking your status from when I came in. I'm here if you need me. After all you've done for me especially freshman year. Thanks for keeping that between you and me.

Airicka: No problem. You think if Miz knew that would change things a little. Not that I would.

Chris: Keep it on locks man. She can never find out.

At the same time Chris is coming out of Airicka's room Mysary comes in the front door. Unsure of what is really going on and too tired to argue Chris retires to his room. Coming up the stairs keys jingling she notices the last seconds of light as Chris' door closes slowly. Hearing the music coming from Airicka's room and seeing the light from

228

Chris's room Miz realizes they are still awake. The general feeling is tonight is not the night to put up with Airicka's lifetime drama. After a shower and a change into some comfortable sweats, Mysary can see that Airicka is still awake. Knocking on her door softly not trying to make too much noise. Airicka invites her in. Before they get into a discussion about what is wrong Airicka who can no longer watch Christopher and Mysary be at odds. In a moment of desperation Airicka tells Mysary what Christopher did two years ago. The wait of the sentiment causes Mysary to look at his door and wonder...

Miz: Why would anybody do something like that for me? What did he think would happen? I mean he had to know that if I found out what it would mean, what does this mean?

As if all at once the barriers around her heart broke from the revelation and those hidden things even in her subconscious, thoughts rush to the front like a wild windstorm.

Airicka: Look, I'm only telling you this because the two of you have not been the friends they used to be. It's really made living here impossible, the silence, avoidance, the...

Miz: And to think all this time I thought he was an ass. He must think I'm the ass now.

Airicka: I thought you and Derik patched things up?

Miz: We did.

Airicka: So why does this even matter? I guess you two needed to patch things up before the wedding Saturday.

Miz: But it was Chris who talked me into working things out with Derik. Shit!

Airicka: Well you know what this sounds like don't you?

Miz: I'm not thinking about what this sounds like. I'm thinking about what this is.

Airicka: Well, what is it?

Miz: I wish I could explain it myself. I'm even more confused now. I got to go to work.

Airicka: You alright?

Mysary unable to come back with one of her many standards I'm okay remarks; she is really lost in thought about what to do with all that she knows now. On top of it all she still doesn't know that Chris and Mai have not spoken in about two weeks. Even though Chris showed himself strong it was all he could do to keep from breaking down in front of Miz. Yes she is his best friend, they can talk and have talked about everything but somehow this is all different now. The only way to explain it is **"This"** *Once you can effectively define "This" true feelings will be locked away and no one will say anything. The night air swelled as her eyes embraced the weight of such a sacrifice. I mean how could he…*

Everything up to this point was so clear. Of course I wanted more but we couldn't. I mean a 12-year friendship is at stake. Not to mention now our commitments. You know I never thought that life could be this complicated. We never kissed before and now there are looks and questions are constantly echoing in my mind. I know it was done in a moment of anger and confusion but this wasn't no moment of weakness this was some stuff that was deep inside. And why did you respond, is this something you wanted all along. I know why I didn't say anything why didn't you...

Today Christopher and Maya planned to go dinner at Tio Pepe's then they would go for a stroll around the lake just to talk. Things have been a little strange between them since the double date with Mysary and Derik. Christopher thinks the change in the air has to do with the last time they had an argument over the car and him leaving to help a friend. Maya is unsure now of what to feel or if she should tell Christopher about Derik. Would you tell your new man that your old boyfriend is currently dating his best friend who you think he has feelings for? When past loves come back into your life even for a second you often find yourself entertaining thoughts of well you fill in the blank. Even though the initial joy of a new relationship has worn-off with Christopher they have bonded well. Maya has opened her heart to trust again, Christopher has made it a point to consider the fears and show simply how beautiful love can be. The trade off has been Christopher has found someone he can openly call his own, Maya can purge her heart of doubt and believe in what love offers. The cozy downstairs restaurant is lit to perfection for a romantic night. Kevin Mahogany's rendition of All Blues is marinating the room as the sounds of lite conversations and the clanking of glasses simmers and blends with the aroma of the evening's dinner choices. Sitting off in the corner, the waiter brings them water and two glasses of their new plum wine. Almost as if timed perfectly, they are ready to order.

Christopher: We'll start with Mediterranean seafood coktail with the fresh fruit.

Waiter: Excellent choice. We just received our fruit order in today. Did you want to order your entrees now? I only ask because most people don't want me to keep coming back and forth interrupting their dinner. And I am usually a good judge of when you need something.

Maya: Really. I'm impressesd.

Christopher: Yeah and it takes a lot to impress her. So if you can pull that off you are really doing something.

Maya giving the eye as if to say I'ma get you when the waiter leaves. Christopher notices and quickly draws indirect attention to her by

Christopher: Well sweetie, shall we order?

Before the waiter could even notice her contenance changes with a gentle lick of her lips ...

Maya: Sure. Not sure which to try the Silver Salmon. Which is better with the Bernaise or the Hollandaise?

Waiter: Me personally, I like it with the Bernaise because the salmon is broiled and the Bernaise just gives it that perfect touch.

Maya: You sold me on it.

Waiter: ...And for you sir?

Christopher: I'll have the Rockfish in the champagne sauce.

Maya: Ooo that sounds good.

Christopher: Could you make sure you bring and extra saucer please.

Maya: Why?

Christopher: Please, you know why?

Waiter: (with a small chuckle) anything else?

Christopher: That will be all for now.

Turning his attention to Maya

Christopher: So?

Maya: Yeah.

Christopher: Tell me. Did you see us making it this far?

Maya: Where have we've made it?

Christopher: C'mon you know most relationships don't make it 3 good months and here we are close to a ½ year.

Maya: yeah and?

Christopher: So you just knew we would be here?

Maya: You didn't?

Christopher: Well I hoped we would, but I wasn't too sure sometimes.

Maya: Why?

Christopher: Let's not get into that part now I'm just really gald we are here.

Maya: Me too.

Appetizer then the main course included with great small talk and another glass of wine, a simple night out is made wonderful. Looking at one another she thinks tonight could be the perfect night to do it. Christopher can't deny the fact that Maya is perfect for him. Yet in all that is perfect there is but one flaw, Mysary. Smiling at Maya as she looks at him with such intent he lets the thought of Mysary fade and really begins to enjoy Luv.

Instead of dessert they agree to get something from the coffee shop near the lake. The night air was unusually cool. The simmer of the lake and the summer breeze so late in the year were more than enough to provide background for a mid evening stroll.

Maya: So what should we do now?

Christopher: I'm just enjoying the night. My plan was dinner and a stroll.

Maya: Well, what do you have to do tomorrow?

Christopher: Nothing much why?

Fearing rejection again she declines to finish her thought.

Maya: Nothing. No reason. Nevermind.

Christopher: Ok, that was weird.

Maya: What?

Christopher: Nothing. Hey look at that.

Maya: What?

Christopher: Those stars over there.

Standing behind her pointing to Aquarius the aroma of his Chrome Legend body oil and the comfort of is arms sends a warm chill through her body. Eyes close she leans into him just to feel his chest on her back, caught up she tilts her head exposing her neck. Chris squeezes Maya breathes, they stand there at the cusp of something. Kissing her neck slowly he realizes this could go too far. Trying to stop, her hands reach up and caress his neck. Maya turns her head, looks into Christopher's eyes she can only see glimmer of the night-lights in his retina. Kissing him the cold soft passion grabs him making the thought of backing out a distant memory. Now face to face the kiss, the embrace takes on a new meaning. The lake and the beauty of the night provide the soundtrack to intimacy. As if the moment could be any less perfect his phone rings. Stopping mid the second ring to see who it is...

Maya: Are you serious?

Christopher: What? (Putting the phone away)

Maya: This right here. You stop because your phone was ringing, are you serious?

Christopher: Is it that deep?

Maya: What do you think?

Christopher: Honestly, I didn't think you would flip like this.

Maya: Flip like what?

236

Christopher: Like this. All because I checked my phone.

Maya: It's not just the phone. I mean every time we get into something you always got to answer your phone or leave and I'm sick of it.

Christopher: What? How you sound?

Maya: You don't get it do you?

Christopher: Get what? (*Getting a little angry.*)

Maya: That I am not important to you.

Christopher: Are you serious?

Maya: You're not funny.

Christopher: I'm not trying to be. I know you not acting a fool on this.

Maya: Are you calling me a fool?

Christopher: Are we in the same conversation?

Maya: What is that supposed to mean?

Christopher: I never called you a fool. Where do you get this everytime thing from, it happened twice.

Maya clearly frustrated, but not like normal, it's as if everything from the past came to the surface all at once. Christopher at this point has no clue where all this is comng from, thinking that the past stuff was resolved and forgotten. So now he is forced to not only defend his current stance but to protect against the sneak attack from some old conflict.

Maya: Whatever Christopher. The question still remains

Christopher: What question is that?

Maya: How important am I to you?

Christopher: So the past 5 months meant nothing?

Maya: That's not what I'm saying

Christopher: Then please explain this to me like I'm 4 because that is what it's sounding like. Is there something else here?

Maya: It doesn't matter now. But don't try to escape the question.

Christopher: Look, this is crazy, I'm not calling you crazy before you get any ideas. This what we are doing is crazy.

Maya: So what is that your way of saying you want out?

Christopher: WHAT?! Where is this coming from?

Maya: Well you said this, I take it you mean us is too crazy for you now.

Christopher: Whatever. I'm done.

Maya: Well then I guess this is goodbye.

Christopher: Is that it?

Turning to walk away she stops for a moment to comeback and say something. Looking at Christopher standing there, she is hurt, angry, and looking as if she has given up so she says

Christopher: Is that It? (*Not more of a question this time his contenance says so you walking out on this, there is no fight left in you to save us?*)

Maya: Yeah, this is it.

And just like that they are done. No fanfare, no parades. No we can work it out. Nothing. They had managed to end up back where her car was, so he still being the gentlemen made sure she got in and everything was ok. Not following her in person with his eyes, he watches as she takes a few miniutes before she starts the car and pulls away. Rather than call anyone to come pick him up its not that late so Christopher decides to take the bus home, the solitude will give him time to gather his thoughts.

One of the few times Mysary invites Derik over for dinner. With the current state of things she is making an attempt to strengthen or overlook a situation that could be nothing more than active imagination. There is still the white elephant in the room, Christopher but this is the right thing to do. I mean, four years in is a long time to throw it away what could be right? Not much of a domestic on the stay at home type and it's amazing the cooking skills she has picked up from friends. Derik usually does the homecooked meals, Mysary would just assume grab a bite from Crazy John's, Po Shan's or any one of the many chicken box place's from around the city. Woman on the go, got no time to slow down. The menu tonight is a spicy little number [20]Bang Bang Chicken with a green salad. No one else is home so tonight should be kind of special. Opening the door...

Derik: Hey love, how was your day?

Mysary: Pretty good and yours?

Derik: Normal, you know same people same attitudes.

Mysary: Well, go have a seat in the living room.

Derik: What smells so good? (*Wrapping his arms around her trying to get a quick kiss. She leans away looking as if to say stop. Unable to lean any further she gives in to his mild demand with a soft short kiss.*)

Mysary: You will find out soon enough. Now go.

---

[20] Bang Bang Chicken recipe (p. 290)

240

Derik: Aw, c'mon man just a little peak.

Mysary: Not for you mister, go sit and relax.

Derik: My, aren't we aggressive.

Mysary: Look, it's not often I will do this so you better appreciate it and do what I say.

Derik: Yes ma'am.

Mysary goes into the kitchen Derik goes into the living room. There is an opening in the kitchen that allows you to see into the living room so they continue to talk while the aroma tempts the taste buds.

Derik: So what do I owe this treatment?

Mysary: No reason, I just wanted to.

Derik: Ok, so whenever I do something I have to have a reason and when you do something it's just because?

Mysary: Yeah and?

Derik: Nothing. Just making sure I understand the rules.

Coming from the kitchen with a glass of wine handing it to Derik.

Mysary: Well, if you ever doubt consult the ref.

241

Derik: And that would be?

Mysary: Me

Derik: So you're the ref too. Next you are going to tell me you're the one calling the plays.

Mysary: Never that. I just wrote the book on how to play the game.

Back and forth from the kitchen bringing place settings, and other dinner necessities, Mysary finally comes out with two [21]ice cold plates in her hands.

Derik: Wow, this looks great.

Mysary: Thank you (*Sitting legs folded on the sofa in the opposite corner, plate on a pillow over her lap.*)

Derik: Man, this is really good.

Mysary: You say that like this is first time you've tasted my cooking.

Derik: Nothing like that, sweetie. I'm just saying you have really out done yourself here. It looks so simple but it tastes good.

Mysary: Really?

---

[21] Cold plates enhance the taste of a fresh salad. Put in freezer for 10 minutes. Take out just before you plate salad or cold food dish.

Derik: Yeah.

Not that she ever required validation from anyone especially a man but, Derik's comment goes a long way. Listening to some [22]music as they continue to talk and eat.

Derik: So, can I ask you a question?

Mysary: You just did. (*Sound familiar?*)

Derik: We've been together for a while now. I am not trying to beat a dead horse, but why is moving in together a bad idea?

Mysary: It has nothing to do with how long we've been together

Derik: Then what is it then?

Mysary: Like I said before that is a long way from home.

Derik: But we can make a new home.

Mysary: Let me finish

Derik: Sorry

Mysary: Leaving together is not as simple as things are now. We get mad at one another you can go to your house or I could go to mine. We

---

[22] Play "For Real" by Amel Larrieux

have our own space is what I am saying.

Derik: So what you're saying is after all this time we haven't had our share of knock down drag outs?

Mysary: That's just it living together is a whole new set of rules. Say what you will I have yet to see it work.

Derik: Well we could be the first

Mysary trying to escape is really having a time as Derik is tightening his grip.

Mysary: Sure, that will work. Do you remember the time when you and I were on our way to work? Your car broke down so we rode together.

Derik: There were a few times things like that happened.

Mysary: I'm getting to it. We got into an argument over which route to take because we were both running late. You got so mad you almost got out of the car on the expressway.

Derik not remembering the story that way digresses from commenting

Mysary: What happens when we get to that point of wanting to walk out? Not to mention the bills and responsibilities. There is no I want out. Either the bills will be in your name. You know my father ain't having that. And the bills in my name, you are not having that. Even

244

trying to split them if one person leaves then what?

Derik: So there's no way this can work?

Mysary: I'm not saying that. I am just saying the current plan will not.

Derik: Well, what does this mean for us?

Mysary: What do you mean?

Derik: Look, you obviously decided to go to Virginia without me. I'm supposed to stay here and what exactly?

Mysary: That is your call. I never said you couldn't move too. I just said the living together won't work.

Derik: You made it work with Christopher and Airicka.

Mysary: That's different and you know it.

Derik: How?

Mysary: Airicka needed a place freshman year, Christopher and I needed another roommate when we found the house to make things work. We found each other at the right time.

Derik: So you and Christopher were already looking for a place to stay right? The two of you were going to make it work. How are you and I different than you and Chris?

There it is. The question that has so many different connotations; that the only thing heavier is the answer. Mysary backed into that corner finally may have to answer what she has alluded for so long.

Mysary: Now you know that Chris and I are friends nothing more.

Trying a quick defense she misdirects his comment to the "We are just friend zone". Derik fires back with a one two...

Derik: That's just it. Are you saying we are not friends or Christopher is a better man than me?

Mysary: Neither, we are friends. What is this really about?

Derik: I'm just trying to understand how you can live with him for four years and there were no problems and we've been together for four years but the thought of living with me is ludacris.

Mysary: What? I never said that. So your problem is not with me it's with Chris?

Oh my, what a devastating counter, this is turning out to be the heavy weight competition we thought it would be.

Derik: You don't have to, the evidence is quite clear.

Mysary: Really? Are you sure you want to go there?

Derik: We can.

This is taking a turn for the worst. Both competitors are clearly bothered by the other's questions and statements. This is not going to end well. Mysary reaching for her phone pulls up the photo.

Mysary: So then what is clear about this?

Derik: Oh so you spying on me?

Mysary: I have no need to spy on you. Or do I? This was sent to me from someone who saw you and thought I needed to know.

Derik: So what do you want me to say?

Mysary: How about the truth?

Derik: Well you first. Tell me you don't love him. Tell me that I am not the consolation prize.

Mysary: Really? If you felt that way why are you with me? Look when you're with me you are with the best and I only deal with the best. I thought you realized that. I was with you not him. You clearly have more to your story than you are telling me. Your obvious refusal to confirm or deny anything leads me to believe you have a secret, either way you are the one with the issue not me.

Derik unable to respond quickly tries to backup and then go in from a different angle more humble and apologetic. The volcano has been awakened and all you can do is watch this beautiful disaster.

Derik: Ah, look bae I'm just saying. I want us to work and it seems like you have already written us off.

Mysary: So what do you want?

Derik: I know what I want and that is you. What I don't know is what about us.

Mysary: Oh so now it's about us.

Derik: What are you saying? It's always been about us.

Mysary: Really? Where did all of this talk of Christopher come from and let me not forget you and Maya obviously have history.

Derik: Ok Maya and I dated a while ago.

Mysary: And you didn't think I should know that?

Derik: It was in the part that didn't matter

Mysary: This right here doesn't look like it doesn't matter. Clearly there is more to this than you are letting on.

Derik: It was nothing. You are my now. I hope you are my future.

Mysary: So what is that? Some attempt at compassion. Well, I'm tired.

Derik: Of us? Are you saying you are tired of us?

Mysary: Derik, take it how you want. I'm done.

Derik: Just like that?

Mysary: What do you want from me?

Derik: Nothing. I guess I should go.

Mysary: Yeah, there's nothing left here.

The dichotomy of the statement renders him speechless. Mysary never one to mince words knew exactly what she was doing. Her pain of being lied to and the fact that Luv has its claws the past and present she can only be protective of her emotions. Derik now a not so innocent casualty collects what he can and leaves.

About a week later after few rounds of phone tag Christopher and Maya meet at the Double T on Route 40. Christopher waiting goes through a list of possible scenarios and comebacks. A crowd of new customers comes in and in anticipation Christopher looks to see if Mai is among them. Disheartened he begins to think that she's probably not coming. He thinks of all the times he has rejected her advances and how elusive he has been when it comes to intimacy. Before he could entertain any more thoughts she comes and sits across from him without taking off her coat.

Christopher: Hey, thanks for coming.

Mai: Yeah

Waitress: Would you like to order now?

Christopher: Mai?

Mai: Nothing for me.

Christopher: Give us minute, please.

Waitress: Sure hon, I'll be back shortly?

Mai disenchanted by the situation looks in every direction except in the one that matters. She stares out the window to punish Christopher by giving him a small part of her attention. He is torn just wanting her to listen to him.

Christopher: Let me start by saying, I'm sorry about the other day.

Mai: Don't do that. The world doesn't need any more sorry men. We got enough of those already. No, you made everything perfectly clear. You just want to be friends and that is okay with me...

Christopher: Would you let me finish first...

Mai: What are you going to say? You don't want me in that way and I'm cool with that. I have enough trouble with Deja. I don't want or need any one who is not ready for me. I knew eventually things would prove to good to be true ...

Christopher: Mai, I've never had sex before.

Mai: Right. Whatever dude.

Christopher: No joke. I never really knew how to tell you. I mean we always were having such a good time it didn't seem like something we needed to talk about. I thought we would have talked about it after the reservoir incident. You wanted to let it go so I did. You were one of the only women…

…Without detection she pretends her phone is ringing. Holding it up to her ear she holds the greatest of phony conversations.

Mai: (*on her phone with one finger silencing Christopher*) Hey, what's up? I'm in the middle of something right now; can it wait til later? Alright then I'll be there shortly. Look I have to go. I'll call you. *Standing with her and trying to stop her before she leaves Chris can only watch helplessly as the pain begins to sink deeper. Playing everything back in his head over and over again he can't understand how things could have gotten so jacked up. Later that day Chris goes to the gym to work off some steam but his mind cannot focus on anything. It seems that if all at once every failed relationship explodes from inside leaving a path of destruction that his mind and heart have become expendable casualties. With all that he had ever learned about women and the way he could create arenas of physical and mental strength to persuade even the most resistant; he was still an amateur. These are those times when you contemplate the importance of the choices you've made and the argument raised to give in rarely sees any opposition. Deep in the recesses of the mind plots and schemes of how, where and when unfold with the utmost clarity and fueled by the desire and anger of deprivation remorse is overshadowed by the thought that* *this may not make things right but it will at least make it even.*

[**Christopher**] This had to be one of those terrible, horrible, no good, very bad days. You know how it is when you wake up still with some heaviness from the night before and you are not sure what or where it is from you just know it's there. I mean for real can I get a do over?

A few days have gone by, Airicka has been coming past to get any mail that is still being delivered and pick up anything she might have left behind. Really she misses Christopher and Mysary so she uses the mail as a reason to chill and talk it up with whoever is home. For the most part Chris is there the most during the day packing up. Before his trip he decided to put most of his stuff in storage and stay with Sam until he ships out.

Airicka just left, Chris is getting back to taking inventory of the stuff you have and the things you should have gotten rid of years ago. Now I could say it started with all the greatest of intentions and then you find that picture, that box, that one thing that stops you in the middle of what some would call utter chaos. Here we find letters and different journal entries that all but give a little insight into the past twelve years. Somehow blended with theses memories are notes and messages from the past few months. With everyone text messaging and chatting it is amazing that people still want to write anything any more. Of course by now you realize its time to read some of these notes that will not be thrown away. What you are about to read are letters and notes from different women some you will know and others you will not but take it from me they are all equally as important to the development of this story.

252

July 28, - *Christopher has always found solace in his writing. He has a collection of journals filled with thoughts poems, song ideas and doodles. The freedom has come at a cost there has been no resolution except the fact his feelings are now on paper.*

September 11, - *Mysary spent junior year of high school away in a college exchange program for gifted athletes. Of course Chris and Miz do the pen pal thing, yeah they could have emailed each other but they had been writing letters since grade school. It's something about the feel of paper and hand written correspondences that mean so much.*

It's amazing how one person's presence even for brief moments in time could make a house feel warm and small. With the way things had been going everything is so amplified. Christopher, sitting in his room working on plans for the concert trying desperately trying to keep his mind off the weights bearing down on his mind and heart. It's like you get those moments when everything is going so good you get caught up and forget the things that are bothering you until they show up right in front of you. This is one of those rare times when Chris has his guard down and can't fully get it up when he hears Mysary coming in the house. The sound of her approaching echoes making it hard to focus. She says nothing as she ascends to the top of the stairs. Her footsteps continue beyond her door but at a much slower pace. Quickly Chris tries to resume his work without looking like he noticed her coming in. Standing in the doorway she leans softly against the door, hands behind her back. She waits until he looks at her...

Miz: Hey, I come in peace. (*Showing a bag from Phillip's*)
Chris placing the pen down shows a look of welcomed apprehension.

253

Miz: Can I come in?

Chris: Sure, if you want to.

Miz: How's it going?

Chris: it's going...

Miz: I brought you some lunch and I thought maybe we could talk?

They both try to ease into the moment without too much emotion on their sleeves. When really they are dying to start back when it was fun. She sitting on the edge of his bed, he turns around in his chair as she opens the cartons revealing black linguine with clams and peppered shrimp and steamed rice. The memory of that night on the Harbor when they both left the ring dance without their drunk or freaky dates and met on the merry-go round to escape the drama comes back. The thought brings about a smile of how bad things had been but their friendship endured. The food serves as more than just a peace offering. It was the catalyst that began the healing process.

Chris: Thanx, So what did you want to talk about?

Miz: We haven't really talked and I really needed to talk to someone. The other day I found this...

Handing Chris a wrinkled laminated card. This coupon entitles the holder to one true friend. Show this card to the giver and feel free to bare your soul and the friend will give you a shoulder or two if necessary.

Chris: Wow! I didn't even think you still had this.

Miz: If you notice there is no expiration date.

Chris: You got it. I always honor my commitments. So which would you like first the left or right?

Offering both shoulders, Mysary laughing gently between tastes.

Chris: Its been a long time since I've seen you smile like that. It's still good to see.

Miz: I just want to say...

Chris: Don't. We both said and did some...

Miz: No let me finish.

Chris: Aight.

Miz: I just wanted to say I hope we can be friends again.

Chris: We never stopped on my end. (*She looks with that will you let me finish please glance*) My bad, continue.

Miz: I think I made a big mistake, (*pausing for the on coming interruption, but it never comes.*) I broke it off with Derik...

Now waiting for some type of response hoping he will be the Chris of old. Ready at the drop of a hat to swoop in with just the right thing to say. And like a true champion in a downward spiral Chris asks.

Chris: What happened? I mean you were so happy together.

**To you the reader i know you are thinking BULLSHIT!
just keep reading.**

Christopher as bad as he may want to say baby I'm yours. He takes one look at her sitting there and thinks to himself not like this. So he plays the role of friend and comforter. Mysary can never let on that she knows what Christopher did for her. Airicka promised to never tell but that could only last for so long between girlfriends. Mysary now has trouble trying to decide between what she feels and what she has wanted all this time.

Miz: Yeah, we were but it seems the closer we got to me leaving the more complicated things became.

Chris: Bull.

Christopher never tells that he and Maya aren't together. Pride will not fall for that.

Miz: What?

Chris: You heard me, pure Bull. Now, are you going to tell me what's really going on? How you let things get complicated to the point you can't uncomplicate things.

Miz: I'm just tired of the complications.

Chris: Oh so is that why we never (*of course this was said under his breath*)

Miz: What? Why do I have to be the one to uncomplicate things. I'm tired Chris.

Chris: Weren't you the one who always told me when you get tired is when you have to put in the most effort to make it work. Is it worth it?

Miz: You are not allowed to use my words against me.

Chris: Ok so tell me do you luv him?

As normal as things seem there is still a huge white elephant in the room, both are for the moment choosing to ignore it but you know it's there. To bury his feelings the only way he knows how, he quickly takes the aggressive approach hoping to bring out the fire of confrontation to douse the luv aching to come out.

Chris: Yo, you bring up you want to talk but you leaving out something.

Mysary too overwhelmed to respond can only cry. Abandoning his original stance Chris can only do what he does best be a friend. With every tear that falls a part of his heart burns slow. Enduring the pain

257

to comfort a friend is all that can be done and it is the catalyst that brings on the flood. But with a bit a resistance Mysary holds back until his voice blends into her mind and nothing can stop the tears.

Miz: I'm sorry, you know I don't do the crying thing (sniff) I have something to show you.

Pulling out her phone showing the picture of and Maya hugging and looking as if they are about to kiss.

Miz: About few weeks ago Neecie sent this to me. I didn't want to send it to you until I found out what it meant.

Chris: And?

Miz: Well that is what started the change in things. Did you see the way they looked at each other when we went out together?

Chris: No. What did I miss?

Miz: I thought nothing of it but I did catch it. So I asked about it when we left. He said it was nothing. Said that they had seen each other before recently and the look was wow small world. You tell me what you think?

Chris upset now because he feels like her breaking it off with him was so she could get with Derik . It doesn't make sense though and then like a flash it hits him like a ton of bricks.

Chris: What do you know about his ex?

Miz: Not much? It was almost 4 years ago. Why, you think he and Maya used to date?

Chris: I'm almost sure of it.

Miz: How can you be so sure?

Chris: Well, we talked and she told me about her last real relationship and how bad it ended. She said it was about 4 years ago. I mean think about it. That would be a reason for the look at dinner you saw. It doesn't explain this picture though.

Miz: So what you going to do now?

Chris: Not sure, she broke it off with me a few weeks ago too.

These words like freedom break loose a dance in Mysary's heart. For the first time since sophmore year in high school the two are not attached or obligated to anyone. Will he? Will she? Should they?

Mysary: You ok?

Christopher: It is what it is?

Mysary: Look at us

Christopher: Yeah this is pretty sad

Mysary: I'm not sad. I have an internship waiting for me.

Christopher: I never said we were sad I said this is sad.

Mysary: What?

Christopher: We've been through some crazy stuff.

Mysary: Yeah, you remember the night we went to junior prom in Mr. Earl's Caddy.

Christopher: Do I. The smell of CK1 and Mad Dog 20/20 still make me laugh. We had a good time though right?

Miz: Yeah, till our dates, left with each other.

Chris: They wanted to knock them boots

Miz: Yeah and I was not having it. Plus I was spanking that ass in bowling all while in my dress

Chris: Oh so you think you can take me

Miz: Ain't nothing here between us, except space and opportunity.

Chris: Well, let's go.

Miz: Now you know it's too late by the time we get there it will be closed.

Chris with his hands out as if to say bring it on. That same pose in the Micheal Jackson "I'm Bad" Video.

Chris: Thought not.

Mysary: What don't get brand new.

Getting up in Christopher's face like they are about to play fight. They laugh and then hug.

Chris: Ah, man I miss this so much

Miz: Miss what?

Christopher: Us man. I miss this right here.

Mysary of course savouring the mental comfort squeezes tight as if his body was life support and any sign of space would be the death of her.

Mysary: (*In a soft and gentle whisper eyes closed*) Oh, Derik.

Christopher: What...did...you call me?

Mysary, with a stone face and a lake of sorrow in her eyes says nothing.

Christopher: That's what I thought you said.

Mysary: Sorry. I guess he's not out of my system.

Christopher: Well I guess it's better than the alternative

Mysary: Whats that?

Christopher: That... Ah hell with it.

Grabbing Mysary by the arm as she tries to turn away then around her waist. His arms lift her slightly hands strong support her side. She is totally taken by surprise and when they kiss for what was the first time, it's like a penthouse suite on cloud nine. Despite being called by his name Christopher could not let her go with out staking his claim to her. Erasing any thought of Derik he engraves his name in this moment and her heart forgets its simple rhythm. They let go as if both needed to give way for air, eyes touch and he asks

Christopher: Who am I?

Mysary: Christopher

Christopher: That's what I thought you meant.

The command in his voice, the confidence in his stature is electric. As if the man in him assured the woman in her who was in control. And like every woman you want a man to be sure of himself.

It's been one of those days when you have this feeling something good is about to happen. Renee comes home to where Airicka is usually waiting with the perfect greeting. Coming in the house as usual Renee doesn't notice the suitcases packed. Talking to Airicka who is not

262

responding because she is upstairs in the closet gathering the last of her things.

Renee: ...Sweetie, I just wanted to say I'm sorry about the other night can we talk about it over dinner or something, Baby I thought we could go out and get something to eat and talk things over. Baby, baby you here?

When the calls go unanswered she begins to look around the house as if it is a game of hide and seek until Airicka comes down the stairs with a bag in hand. At the same time, Renee notices the suitcases in the front.

Renee: Wait a minute, what's all this?

Airicka: I decided to take the internship Upstate?

Renee: So you moving?

Airicka: After last night I see that we are going in different directions and it's best if I go.

Renee: What? We can't talk about it? I gave up a lot for this. You could at least give me that.

Airicka: The last time I had an offer to intern I turned it down. You know why, it was because of you. All my life I've been doing things for others with the hope of being accepted by them. Never once taking care of my own needs. This right here ain't about you, so before you try that routine of what I owe, pay it forward because all my debts are cancelled.

Renee: Are you mad at me? I just wanted to talk.

Airicka: Nah I ain't mad. I know if we talk you will just convince me to stay.

At that moment Brevin pulls up and beeps the horn. Not even trying to start static Airicka ends everything with just a kiss on the check and...

Airicka: Look that's my ride. I'm sorry.

Walking out of the door Renee stands and tries to make some kind of sense of what just happened. Stunned as all this was a shock she never thought that what went on last night would upset her that much. Thinking about what could have been, the only thing she can say is

Renee: I'm sorry too.

The small echoes of a late day peak through the rafters and other openings as the somber lights of the room match the sentiment of the group. Unable to really get anything accomplished Chris needs a breather. No one in the group really knows what is going on with him they all notice there has been a dramatic change in his demeanor. Returning from the corner store with drinks and things, Sam looks for Chris.

Sam: Where did he go?

Tischa: After snapping at everyone he stormed out that door in the back. Do you have any idea what the hell is going on with him? Why is he acting so foul?

Dynah: I have never seen Chris act like this before. I mean I know things haven't really gone as planned but we all lost a little something here.

Daniel: Yo Sam, I'm not for all this drama. I went through that before with the last group I was with. I know I'm new and all but for real I'm about ready to bounce.

Sam: D, man if that's what you gotta do then do that. I'm not going to say that you won't be missed, because you will. You have been one of the best violinists we've ever had and this right here is just one of those times when a group has to put in work. Know what I'm sayin? We put this group together for more than just a sound. It has been a pact that we are in this for the long haul. If anybody at anytime wants to leave they're more than welcome to. As a group, we all promise to stand with one another, if one member is hurt we all hurt. Chris has been here since the beginning. Danny, remember when you were in trouble and couldn't find anybody to help? Who was there? Tisch and Dynah, now you know that we have all had our day, week, month or year of dismay.

Dynah: Yeah, I see what your saying it's just hard to see a brother like this, you know.

Sam: I'll be back. I'll see what I can find out. Let's just call rehearsal for the day, a'ight.

Going out onto the roof, Sam looks around before noticing Chris sitting on the ledge sort of off in a daze. Not quick to ask about what happened more concerned about getting information about what has been going on with him.

Sam: You a'ight man?

Chris: Yeah (*with a low distant tone*)

Sam: Are you sure?

Chris: What you a mind reader now?

Sam: You could say that I mean Cleo is out of business somebody needs to pick up the slack. So what is it?

Chris: You know other than you, Miz, nobody knows the real me. That is kind of scary.

Sam: Well you and Mai seem to be hittin' it off?

Chris: On the real, I thought she was different. I thought I could talk to her...

Sam: Oh no, you told her the truth. You didn't? What did she say?

Chris: She thought I was lying. Ragging about me looking hard sayingI've sent mixed messages and shit. She thought that, you know I don't know what she thought but that ain't the half, her ex is Derik.

Sam: Yo Miz's Derik?

Chris: Fa Sho'

Sam: Does she know?

Chris: Yeah she showed me a recent picture of them hugged up. Maya told me about her last relationship was 4 yrs ago then I put 2 and 2 together and it came up them. Talk about real fucking weird.

Sam: When did this happen?

Chris: That night we decided to double date. Mai and I were late getting there; she had trouble getting someone to watch her sister. So when we got there, they were already waiting. When Derik and Mai saw each other I don't know, it was something odd there about that moment but I just passed it off as nothing you know. After that Miz and I hadn't seen too much of each other and it seem like we got mad for no reason.

Sam: So what did she say when you asked her?

Chris: I never got the chance to say anything.

Sam: Why not?

Chris: We broke it off. Well, she did the breaking, I was just left broken. Like I said man I just knew she was different than the rest.

Sam: So how did Miz deal with it?

Chris: On the one hand she told that same day and didn't wait a week. She said she wanted me to know. That felt good that she was in to me like that.

Sam: On the other hand...

Chris: Yo, I feel like this just makes things uncomfortable. I don't know why I just do.

Sam: So what you gonna do?

Chris: I don't know man I really care about her and I was finally ready to make that step.

Sam: We are still talking about Maya, right?

Chris:...yeah who did you think?

Sam: (*Brushing it off and quickly changing the subject getting back on track about the rest of rehearsal*) Yo everybody inside trying to figure out when the apocalypse was coming. Nobody has ever seen you down like this. So I just canceled the rest of rehearsal.

As if that was the one peace holding him together he breaks all at once.

Simply put the Superman we thought we knew is human after all.

Chris: Honestly I'm tired of being the good guy. I never seem to get what I want or what I need.

There is no way to fully explain this moment in a man's life so I will give you what I can. Society as a whole has put an unfair burden on men and has stacked the deck against him to fail. As a young man, he is conditioned to be tough and competitive, focused only on the goal of being a measured success. He is trained to deal with questions of or about identity in private and although God has given everyone tear ducts a man must never use them. Men are told to be the leader by their mothers but really women don't want men to take charge. Okay 96% don't. Look at our churches, talk shows and media. The messages are "Real men need to step up and do". But no one looks at where the man is hurting from decades of hiding pain. Women are so emotional passing off true transparency for a good cry as healing or deliverance, Society weeps with them and continually crucifies the man.

Every so often a few good prospects come through the crop. These guys fall into one of few categories. The farmer- carefully planting seeds that will eventually produce fruit to cater to the taste of the moment, the Caregiver- Always bearing the weight of everyone else no matter how much it destroys him on the inside. Trying to fill the void of every bad man that has ever done a woman wrong, and the Sellout just wanting to be accepted, he will go to great lengths to set a value to himself. Willing to do anything at the drop of a hat just to feel important. I am not a Doctor nor am I anyone else who tries to fool you into thinking that I have all answers. If this doesn't apply, then it is what it is. I

269

would just ask that you think about the people you have encountered. Do you know who they really are? Did they let you see what they wanted you to see and six months later the real person comes out? Now I could go on to say there are all these other types of men but the truth be told every man, Hell every person just wants to be appreciated, respected,and to just feel like they are not alone. As long as we continue to go through life afraid to expose who we are, we will never find the one.

Christoher refusing to face his own areas of trust, drowns himself in the things he does to escape dealing with the life he created. Which one of us is really ready to leave the comforts of our own unhappiness and go at least one round with who we really are?

It's been a week or so since the official break-ups, in this time you are not really sure how to act. Four years of tradition and systematic rituals are gone. No phone calls, your world never seemed so large and you never felt so small. Everything reminds you of them and everyone else appears to be so much happier than you. You have one last shot at redemption or trying to gain the upper hand. Grabbing all the memories left in his apartment, Derik makes the green mile drive to Mysary. Playing in his head how things will go, what he will say, how she will respond. Trying to make peace with the pain to go away long enough to ...

Opening the front door, even though she did the breaking, there is a joy to see his face. However she must stand to her resolve and not let the moment change her decision.

Mysary: Derik, is everything ok?

Derik: No, not really, but I will be.

Mysary: Ok, what's up?

Wanting to be asked in, wanting him to come in the mental struggle is if I ask will I be giving up too much ground so soon what do I do? Standing at the door looking at one another is too hard so...

Derik: Here.

Mysary: What's this?

Looking in the bag recognizing it was filled with items left at his home she realizes this is it. Handing it to her he hopes this isn't the end.

Mysary: Oh, thank you.

Derik: So this is it?

Mysary: (*Pausing bag in hand, eyes wanting to say no, heart in too much pain to respond. Brain stupidly responds...*) Yes.

Derik: We can't talk this out? Four years. Four years and it ends like this?

Mysary: (*Not wanting confrontation but her heart understanding the*

271

only course of action now is protection from any further damage.)
There is nothing else to say Derik; it is what it is. What is more talking going to do than just make things harder than they already are?

Derik: I just can't believe this is it. I love you.

Mysary: I love you too. But this is not about love.

Derik: Then I'm lost. If we love each other why can't this be fixed?

Mysary: I'm tired.

Derik: What does that mean?

Mysary: I've got to move and be in Virginia within the next two weeks, get myself situated and this thing with us is just a little too much to deal with too.

Derik: I'm willing to fight to make us work.

Mysary: That's just it, you only see the fight not the casualties of war.

Derik wanting clarity but can see the weight of everything in her eyes says nothing. Instead he does what he knows is best, tries to comfort her with a hug. Stretching his arms toward Misery she is first reluctant because the last thing she can take is the safety she feels in his embrace. Then there is that moment when you say, I'm strong enough to resist the temptation and before your mind can say, "What the hell are you doing?" you're there. Wrapped tight every part of her connecting to him like perfection. The thunderstorm of her resistance colliding with sweet surrender of his love, makes the concept of peaceful transition almost impossible. He wants her, she needs him, they somehow convince the air around them to pause as their bodies caress the moment. Not wanting to let go but realizing they have to. Derik is convinced there is still a chance for them. Mysary doubts if she will really be able to escape one last time and then they kiss.

Mysary: No.

Derik: I'm sorry.

Mysary: Derik, you are making this too hard.

Derik: I'm sorry. I should go.

Mysary: I'm sorry.

Dreik: No. Don't be.

Walking away he refuses to turn back, she remembers the pressing of his lips against hers and considers calling him back, but doesn't. It's really over?

Maybe a few days later, Chris is at home alone. Since Airicka left most of the time the two roommates have the house to themselves. Talking to Sam about plans for tomorrow Chris, for the moment is preoccupied from all the craziness that has happened in the past weeks. There's a knock at the door and not even thinking who it could be Christopher tells Sam to hold on and then ...

Mai: Hey.

*The moment he saw her, his brain froze as the memories resurfaced.
With a soft hesitation she looks at him with a smile of peace. With no
sign of verbal response and only the look of content, she makes the first
move.*

Mai: I know I came by unannounced. Do you have to work today?

Chris: Nah, I'm off so I can pack up.

Mai: Oh, so you are going to Africa?

Chris: Yes, there was only one reason I chose to stay, well actually
two.

Mai: So what now?

Chris: I'm not really sure.

Mai: Can I come in?

*As much as he wants to resist, he just can't convince his arms to say
no. His brain screams, "Do not let her in! Do not let her in! Hey
stupid this is only going to end up wrong! Do you hear me?" It's not
our brain that we hear nor is it our dicks to tell the truth the heart is a
mother. Standing there looking pain, pleasure, anger and desire dead*

in the eye, there is a struggle for dominance as the question then shifts to an invitation to just stay here.

Mai: Maybe we can talk out here? Look I know you weren't expecting to see me but I just want to talk.

Chris with head tilted back and to the side, let's out a breath and opens the door. Going onto the porch was not the desired result but she would have to make it work. Cold without any thought of emotion, he refuses the wanting to even look at her.

Chris: Speak on it man.

Mai: Look? (*with hesitation she redirects her approach*) First I want to apologize, I should not have left things the way I did. I know after we had become so close it seemed like out of nowhere I started keeping you at a distance, it's just that... This was so much easier on the way over here.

Chris: You need more time to rehearse?

Lifting his eyes to make sure the shot was deadly accurate. It seemed like that was all it took to break her. Holding back tears trying to recover to lay her heart out there...

Mai: I'm sorry, I know I hurt you by not telling you about me and Derik. But it never seemed to be the right time to fully get into it. I mean he was my past and after seeing him that night it brought back some feelings I thought Iwas finally over. You have to understand what

275

I had been through with him. I told you about it. I was not ready to see him again with someone else even though it had been three and half years. It was a bit too much. Then the whole deal at the resevoir made me feel a little rejected; no it made me feel rejected completely. I didn't know how to handle that. Everything between us seemed so wonderful. I felt like I was ready to move on. I felt like that was the only thing left. When you turned me down I thought you didn't want me. You never made any real passes at me, I mean the virginity thing was a bit much, who does that anymore?

The look of whatever is perceived although Chris still says nothing. Even if he doesn't answer, she has to speak her heart. Clinging to the hope there is something there to save Maya, goes for broke.

Mai: Chris, I've` never had anybody there for me. I mean just for me. You are like no man I have ever had in my life. I constantly waited for the other shoe to drop. I didn't understand when things just kept getting better. Secretly I thought I was part of some game between you and your roommate. I couldn't handle it all. It was too much. I thought your were playing me with that whole virginity thing especially when we talked about the past girlfriends you had. I couldn't believe it. I didn't want to believe it. You have made such a difference in my life these past few months. No one has ever gotten as close to me as you had. I, I, don't know how to say this (*taking a deep exhaling breath*) Christopher Company I, I, L...

Chistopher: Stop. Stop.

For a moment Mai is in limbo as to what he will say next.

276

Christopher: As much as I really want to forget the last two weeks I can't. You and I were building something. I mean I thought since you had the one bad relationship that hurt you so much it would be best if we took things slow. It had something to do with my vow of purity but more to do with what we were working on. I never gave you any reason to think I was anything less than straight with you. Yet and still you were so quick to treat me like my name was Stanley or some other off brand clown. I was upset about the thing and the way you flipped out about me helping Mysary that night. I thought about it though and flipped things around and considered what if the roles were reversed. To some extent I understood your point. I let it go. So I was able to talk to you and apologize for not considering your side.

Mai: So then you understand then why I am here? Making a fool of myself?

Christopher: How can I be sure of that? How can I be sure that this is not the result of regret? Remember when I wanted to talk? You weren't having it. If this one thing could destroy what we put into us; how am I supposed to look at what we had as nothing more than you rebounding?

Mai feeling totally dejected but also feeling as if it's deserved, she can only take it. Chris wanting to be mad and having the right to be realizes Maya loves him. As if God stepped in and said I have forgiven you why can't you forgive her? Like everyone we immediately pull out the laundry list of pain we have suffered at the hands of this person.

Mai: I know, you have every right to be upset with me and I don't blame you for...

277

Chris: Stop. I'm here trying to think of a reason to hate you.

Chris takes the time to show the dying feeling waiting to get out. His heart is very reluctant and his arms are over zealous. The contradiction, a party of compassion and apprehension and the guest is Mai Love. She breaks completely not like a woman helpless in need of a man. She for the first time in her life knows what love is. The weight of someone actually forgiving your immaturity and accepting you when there are so many reasons to turn you away it's a bit overwhelming. Kissing her on the forehead endearing himself to her they stand on the porch locked in each others arms. The breeze; a reminder of their first night together under the stars. The hug now is much tighter that Luv and Company are comfortable again. The pain is still there but the love is like aloe for the bruised soul.

Now in the context of things, they never said this to one another, can we? Blah blah blah. They simply and very intently share a long tender romantic kiss. The longer they kiss the more the meaning and intensions sway from innocent. Things could never really go back to the way they were on either side now. At some point they have to pull away before **"THIS"** *happens. Mai pulls away this time crying a little because she feels bad for what she wants. Chris recognizing the tears but not the reason tries to hug and pulls her back in to him. His quiet strength explodes all around her. Things and situations have started to come up for him as well. Noticing that his nature is rising Maya looks into his eyes and he looks at her. Everything he wants and all of what she needs is sealed in this. Maintaining composure is harder than the*

278

[23] Riemann Hypothesis. She wants him, he needs her, with each move somehow they convince the air to pause.

Maya: I should go

Christopher: I don't want you too

Maya: All the more reason I should before... Well, you may not have regrets but I do.

It was a simple phone call, a visit in a moment of weakness or a time of temptation, call it what you want. It doesn't change what's about to happen. Mysary, Maya, Christopher, and Derik who's calling whom?

---

[23] A little math humor considered as one of the hardest problems ever.

: You called me?

:I shouldn't be here.

: Are we really thinking about doing this?

: You came.

: You sure you want to do this?

: I'm going to…leave, I should go.

: Wait.

:Don't leave?

: I need you.

: Wait.

: Won't you at least come in?

: Can I come in?

:What are we doing?

: We've done nothing.

: Maybe you should go.

:Stay with me.

: It just won't work things

280

are different now.

:Can we ever go back to the
way it was before this?

:I want to kiss you.

:Is it wrong that I want to kiss you?

:What does this all mean?

:Why am I here?

: We're not together.

:Does this mean we're together?

:What about tomorrow?

:Luv me today.

:What if …

:I LUV YOU.

*So here we are. A moment some of you thought would never come. But
who would ever guess these two would be here. You say you saw it
coming. Time has a way of making this seem right. You may ask about
their other obligations. Or like these two at this point it's a lost cause.*

I only have one request now as you read this play the track entitled
"Body Heat" as you read...

You want her and she needs you. Somehow convincing the air to pause as bodies slide between the echoes of silenceSecret to the night passionate whispers and anticipations grind slow as beauty caresses and massages harmony with the true taste of heat.

Tender to the touch this moment foreign to all as the evening lights dim behind the curtains of a passing cloud. in through the eyes a stream of wind dances the mirange' with multi-layered candle flames.

As lips collide nobody could ever believe that it would feel this good. When the stars start to rain and the moon begins to mellow out hands connect gently creating one color, intensity

Fingers persuade clothes to melt in the fleeting shadows while palms of hands inhale the small of the back breathing cries into every pore. Words are being exchanged with the primal rhythms played between heartbeats and pulse.

Each new move quickly understanding the importance of its predecessor adapts a more pleasurable variant.
Finally pressed against caution and danger intermingled remains crash weightless to the pillow top canvas.

Sheets now being smeared like waves aligned with the shore dwell in the flavor of contradiction.
Wrong so opposed to right until the moment they became the statement

of this one night

Everything you want and all of what he needs is sealed in this
Committed to fulfill this; happiness whales from the wall as half of a
millisecond becomes countless hours drifting into the night and often
overlapping one another driving nerves and reservation beyond the
edge of reason.

The sound of blue drips relaxation between fingers that satisfy the
panting of subtle moans

Delight and Joy are now trapped beneath the scent embedded in
cashmere tattoos of lips and tongue that embraceof the body with a soft
raging kiss.

is this real holding tight the way time feels caught up in the dance of
our lips?

Amazing you, me hidden here in what we need promises bent into
shattered certainty.

Strange the danger blooms like a flower in spring and the belief in
beautiful explodes behind the freedom lost in every touch.

With a feverish passion unleashed composure comes undone to the
comprehension of that pleasure point. Tenderness in his voice vibrates
the walls of her building clutch pillows endure the reality lost in the
pages of this fairy tale.
Hands run through hair legs lock around shoulders as even mistakes are

quickly forgiven in this montage of introduction

Even though I am scared you never made me feel more secure patiently
each pore begins to release a parade of tears as you set me free.
Milky soft skin drowned in honey engulfs me as our bodies, candles,
and the room burn.

Moments can only inhale as fingers linger all around finding new ways
to draw from you

Desire is nourished in the river of ease the music made redefines the
rhythm and pattern of trust. As the stars peek through the window we
both wonder if this is real

The deeper i get inside you i never want to leave. In exchange for you
taking my body slowly i dive into your soul

Why did this take so long? This is too good to be right for either of us.

Baptized in the liquid words of you I can only relish in this stolen
period in time. Outside commitments are of no concern tomorrow's
secrets can't be kept until they are complete.

I can't believe the breakthrough feels so natural like this was meant to
be tonight we make…

Love lust who gives a damn the height of this feeling causes my body
to beat over time swallowed by this you push and pull slowly
syncopating your attacks and taking control of even my basic

movements.

Looking down at you kissing your thoughts with my eyes there is no point of reference of where this began or when it will end the burning cold sweat creates a glow that accents your beauty even more.

Our bodies lost deep in the exhaustion of heavy conversation drift to a place where joy is perfected before it is sent out as a verbal description of anything.

The sun begins to croon the newness of a fresh day as the kisses of morning lay remembered across the bulbs of tulips and mums...

…Now that we're done what are you thinking?

Signature Recipes from the story

DESSERTS AND APPETIZERS
Lady T's

2 cups white chocolate chips

2 tablespoons shortening

In 1-quart saucepan combine white chocolate chips and shortening.
Cook over low heat, stirring occasionally, until melted and smooth
(3 to 5 minutes).
Take paper cups and place in mini cupcake holder for stability.
Pour melted mixture evenly into cups. Place cups in freezer for 3 hours.

Sweet Meatballs

2 lbs. ground turkey

1/4 tsp. garlic powder

1/2 tsp. seasalt

1/4 tsp. Cyanne Pepper

1/2 Cup seasoned or Italian Bread Crumbs

1 grated onion

Sauce ingredients

6 oz. Apricot Preserves

Jar of Chunky Mushroom Tomato sauce

Mix together the above ingredients and form into small meatballs.
Bake meatball in oven until brown. Drain off juice from meatballs.
Mix the following sauce ingredients in a pan and simmer for 5 minutes:
Add the meatballs, cover and simmer for 1 hour, stirring occasionally.

Pickled Cucumbers

1/2 peck cucumbers

1 Cup Ice Cold water

2 Cups Apple Cider vinegar

1/3 Cup of Sugar

Mix water, vinegar and sugar in a large bowl until sugar dissolves. Slice cucumbers a quarter of an inch thick. Place cucumbers in the mix and stir. Make sure cucmbers are completely covered. Refrigerate for 24 hours.

Rock-a-fella Mushroom Recipe

1lb. White Mushroom caps

4 Slices Turkey Bacon

1/4 Cup chopped red onion

Fresh spinach

1/4 Cup of grated Parmesan Cheese

1 tablespoon Tarragon

1/3 Cup of margarine

Crushed Red peppers

Lemon slices and lemon balm for garnish

Take fresh spinach rise thoroughly. Mince cut the leaves by hand or food processor. Combine red onion, spinach in a lg. bowl. in a medium sauce pan melt margarine on low heat (1 to 2 minutes). Add margarine to mixture and blend with fork. While mixing add tarragon and tabasco. Let stand for 2-3 minutes to stiffen. Fill caps with mixture. Cut bacon into 1" pieces place on top and sprinkle on parmesan cheese hold in place with a wooden toothpick. Place in a baking dish bake for 3-5 minutes at 400 degrees on top rack. Serve hot with lemon garnish.

Cookies N' Crème Cupcakes

1 cup soy milk

1 teaspoon apple cider vinegar

3/4 cup Sugar

1/3 cup canola oil

1 teaspoon Vanilla Extract

1/2 teaspoon almond extract, chocolate extract, or more vanilla extract

1 cup all-purpose flour

1/3 cup cocoa powder, Dutch-processed or regular

3/4 teaspoon baking soda

1/2 teaspoon baking powder

1/4 teaspoon salt

Preheat oven to 350°F and line a muffin pan with paper or foil liners. Whisk together the soy milk and vinegar in a large bowl, and set aside for a few minutes to curdle. Add the sugar, oil, vanilla extract, and other extract, if using, to the soy milk mixture and beat until foamy. In a separate bowl, sift together the flour, cocoa powder, baking soda, baking powder, and salt. Add in two batches to wet ingredients and beat until no large lumps remain (a few tiny lumps are OK).

Pour into liners, filling 3/4 of the way. Bake 18 to 20 minutes, until a toothpick inserted into the center comes out clean. Transfer to a cooling rack and let cool completely.

Entrees

Fusili Pomodoro

1lb. Fusilli Pasta

2lbs. Manilla Clams

4 Chopped Parsley Sprigs

4 Cloves Chopped Garlic

1 Pinch Chilli Flakes

1/3 Cup Extra Virgin Olive Oil

In pot of boiling water (with salt) drop linguine and stir.

Into large saute pan, put olive oil, chili flakes, garlic and half of the parsely, roasting garlic to blonde; add white wine.add clams to pan and over with lid. Clams are cooked when all are open. Drain pasta and add to saute pan with the remaining parsley. Stir together & serve

Bang Bang Shrimp or Bang Bang Chicken

1 lb shrimp, shelled and deveined on both sides (*don't butterfly*)

1 lb Chicken Wingettes

1 Tbsp Lite Salad Dressiung

1/4 Cup Thai sweet chili sauce

1/2-3/4 Cup cornstarch, to coat the shrimp in (*elininate if you plan to grill shrimp/chicken, sautee'shrimp or bake chicken*)

Mix salad dressing and sweet chilli sauce. Coat shrimp in cornstarch deep fry untillightly brown. Deep fry wingettes until completely cooked. Drain on paper towel. Toss shrimp/chicken in sauce mixture until coated. Serve on bed of Romaine lettuce.

If sautee or grilling shrimp cook until perfect pink then toss shrimp in sauce mixture and serve.

Black Linguinie Peppers Recipe

4 large garlic cloves, minced a scant

1/4 teaspoon dried hot red pepper flakes

2 tablespoons olive oil

2 orange bell peppers, cut into thin strips

1 red bell pepper, cut into thin strips

3/4 cup dry white wine

1/2 cup chicken broth or water

1/2 pound black linguine, (squid or cuttlefish ink pasta)*

1/3 cup finely chopped fresh parsley leaves

In a 5-quart kettle bring 4 quarts salted water to a boil for pasta. In a 12-inch heavy skillet cook garlic with pepper flakes in oil over moderate heat, stirring, until garlic begins to turn golden. Add bell peppers with salt to taste and cook, stirring, until softened. Add wine and boil, stirring occasionally until almost all liquid is evaporated. Add broth or water and simmer, covered, until bell peppers are tender, about 5 minutes. Pepper mixture may be made 1 day ahead and chilled, covered. Reheat mixture in skillet before proceeding.

In boiling water cook pasta until al dente and drain in a colander. Add pasta to pepper mixture with parsley and toss with salt and pepper to taste over moderate heat until combined well and heated through. Divide pasta mixture among 6 small plates and garnish with parsley

Salmon with Bearnaise Sauce with Dill and Capers

1 Box of pastry sheets

2 Salmon fillets with the skin (no scales)

2 Eggs (beaten)

Juice of 1 whole lemon

4 Tblsp Capers

¼ Cup Parsley

1 Tbsp Dried dill weed

1 Tbsp Tarragon vinegar

Roll out pastry sheets 1/8 inch-thick.

Cut each sheet into 2 squares.

Place one salmon fillet, skin side up, on each pastry square.

Fold pastry around fillet; brush edges with egg and seal.

Place on cookie sheet, seam side down. Brush with beaten egg.

Bake 30 minutes at 350°F until golden brown.

Prepare Bearnaise sauce.

Beat egg yolks and lemon juice until well-blended in the top half of a double boiler.Place over bottom half of double boiler and cook slowly over very low heat, never allowing water to come to a boil.

Add melted butter slowly, stirring constantly with a spoon.

Add capers, parsley, dill, and vinegar.

Stir to blend.

Rockfish with Champagne Wine Sauce (*Recipe is for 4 people*)

2 tablespoons fresh parsley, finely chopped

1/2 teaspoon Old Bay™

1/2 teaspoon dried mustard

2 teaspoons fresh lemon juice

2 tablespoons butter, softened

1 pound fresh jumbo lump crabmeat

4 (6 ounce) fillets rockfish

Preheat oven to 400 degrees F. Lightly grease an 8x8 baking dish.

Mix parsley, seafood seasoning, mustard, pepper, lemon juice, and butter together in a mixing bowl. Gently stir in the crabmeat until well blended, being careful not to break the crab chunks.

Place the fish fillets on a clean surface, and spoon 1/4 of the crab mixture onto one side. Starting on the side with the crab mixture, roll up the fillet around the crab filling. Place the rolled fish into the prepared dish open side down. Bake in preheated oven until light brown and bubbly, and fish flakes with a fork, about 15 minutes.

Champagne Wine Sauce for Rock(optional)

1/2 ounce dried mushrooms

1 Cup chicken or vegetable stock

2 Cups Champagne

1/3 Cup shallots, minced

Unsalted butter, 1/4 cup to add to the sparkling wine, 3 Tbsp for the roux

3 Tbsp all-purpose flour

1 Add the stock and dried mushrooms into a medium sized pot. Cover and bring to a boil, then reduce heat to its lowest setting.

2 In separate medium sized pot, add the sparkling wine and shallots. Bring to a rolling boil, and boil until the wine has reduced to 3/4 of a cup. Turn off the heat and wait until the wine stops simmering, then whisk in 1/4 cup of butter, a little at a time.3 Heat 3 Tbsp butter in a saucepan over medium-high heat. When the butter stops foaming, add the flour and stir well to combine. Stirring often, cook this roux for 5 minutes, or until it turns the color of coffee-with-cream

Drinks

Cranberry Lemonade Punch

5 Cups water, divided

1/2 Cup sugar

1 (6-ounce) can frozen lemonade concentrate, thawed

3 Cups cranberry juice

Stir together 2 cups water and sugar in a small saucepan over medium heat, stirring until sugar dissolves.

Stir together sugar mixture, thawed lemonade concentrate, cranberry juice, and remaining 3 cups water. Chill until ready to serve.

Blue Magic Recipe (Graduation party drink)

1/2 oz Blue Curacao liqueur

1/2 oz Peach liqueur

1/2 oz amaretto almond liqueur

1 part cranberry juice

Pour ingredients into a mixing cup one-quarter filled ice. Stir, and pour into a shot glass. Graduation version served in a tube

Day at the Beach Recipe (serves 4)

4 oz coconut rum

2 oz amaretto almond liqueur

16 oz orange juice

2 oz grenadine syrup

Shake rum, amaretto, and orange juice in a shaker filled with ice. Strain into a highball glass over ice. Add grenadine and garnish with a pineapple wedge and a strawberry.

Poop in the Water (Donte's new shot)

1/2 oz Blue Curacao liqueur

Splash of Sweet & Sour Mix

½ Tootsie Roll

Pour ingredients into shot glass place tootsie roll in last. Let the conversation begin.

I Can Drink Some Shit (Donte's new drink)

1/2 oz. Vodka

1/2 oz. Cranberry Juice

1/4 oz. Amaretto

1/4 oz. Chambord

1/4 oz. Rum (preferably Malabu)

1/4 oz. Midori

1/4 oz. Pineapple Juice

Pour ingredients into a mixing cup one-quarter filled ice. Shake, and pour into collins glass.

Cape Cod Tea Recipe (Christopher & Mai's Drink)

1 Piece fresh gingerroot or 2 - 4 Cinnamon Sticks

5 Cups Water

1/2 CupsWater

4 Orange wheels

1/2 Cups Sugar

3 oz Cranberry juice

10 Green tea (unbleached teabags)

Peel gingerroot and cut into thin slices. Boil water, sugar and gingerroot/ Cinnamon Sticks until the sugar dissolves. Let cool. Brew the 10 teabags in 5 cups water and let it cool. For each serving, place 2 orange wheels, 1-ounce ginger syrup, 4 ounces brewed tea and 3 ounces cranberry juice in an ice-filled mixing glass. Shake and strain into ice-filled wine glass or tumbler. Garnish with additional orange wheels

Cape Cod Cooler Recipe (Alcoholic Version)

2 oz sloe gin

1 oz gin

5 oz cranberry juice

1/2 oz fresh lime juice

1/2 oz orgeat syrup

Pour the gins, cranberry juice, lime juice & orgeat syrup into a cocktail shaker ½ -filled with ice cubes. Shake well. Strain into a collins glass ¾ filled with ice cubes. Garnish with a slice of lime,serve.

Cherry Fucker Recipe (Brevin's Intro Drink to Airicka)

1/2 oz Chambord raspberry liqueur

1/2 oz Peachtree schnapps

1/2 oz cranberry juice

1/2 oz vodka

Pour all ingredients in a mixing tin over ice, stir, and strain into shot glass.

Shake That Ass (Brevin's 2nd Intro Drink to Airicka)

3/4 oz Blue Curacao liqueur

3/4 oz Banana liqueur

3/4 oz Sweet & Sour

3/4 oz Oranges

Build in a shot glass.

Porn Star

1/2 oz Blue Curacao liqueur

1/2 oz Chambord raspberry liqueur

Pour all ingredients in a mixing tin over ice, stir, and strain into shot glass.

Dedication

To Kenya C. Gee, for the memories on Reisterstown Rd., Mc Culloh St., Lawnview and Linwood—Miss you so much Dirty Bo!

For moreinformation about this and other projects by d.a. funn

Log on to www.mistafunn.com

Follow on facebook: facebook.com/mistafunn.com

Follow on twitter: twitter.com/mistafunn

To everyone involved – THANK YOU